A r ... planet.

Step ... tently
at Wei ... undred
this m ... up an automated navigation
beacon broadcasting at two minute intervals in Neptune
orbit."

"Incredible . . ." Weir muttered. He looked up at Lyle,
at the video wall, at Hollis. His chest felt hollow, but his
heart felt huge and leathery, pounding helplessly in his
chest. "These are the same coordinates as before the ship
disappeared . . . this, this happened?" He swallowed, hard,
trying to force control, trying to grab hold of the scientific
approach before his growing excitement started him shaking. "This isn't some kind of hoax?"

"I wouldn't bring you here on a hoax," Hollis said. Weir
recalled too well that strange and unusual events did not
go over too well with Hollis. "Houston confirmed the
telemetry and ID codes."

Weir took several steps towards Hollis' desk, then one
back, turning to stare at the video wall. "It's the *Event
Horizon*," Weir said, trying to get his breath, trying to force
his heart to slow down. "She's come back."

EVENT HORIZON

by

STEVEN MCDONALD

based on the motion picture screenplay

by PHILIP EISNER

TOR®

A TOM DOHERTY ASSOCIATES BOOK
NEW YORK

This is a work of fiction. All the characters and events portrayed in this book are either products of the author's imagination or are used fictitiously.

EVENT HORIZON

Copyright TM & © 1997 Paramount Pictures, Inc.

Cover art © Paramount Pictures, Inc.

A Tor Book
Published by Tom Doherty Associates, Inc.
175 Fifth Avenue
New York, NY 10010

Tor Books on the World Wide Web:
http://www.tor.com

Tor® is a registered trademark of Tom Doherty Associates, Inc.

ISBN: 0-812-54006-9

First edition: August 1997

Printed in the United States of America

0 9 8 7 6 5 4 3 2 1

Dedication

For my Dad,
Edward Charles "Ted" McDonald,
January 7th 1933–March 26th 1997
He handed me the keys to time and space.

and

For Sylvia, Cherry, and Jim,
who believed
and would not let
"he then sadly fell silent"
be the end of the story.

Prologue

Space is deep.

Floating down through night, this thought came unbidden, shot across confusion. The darkness was impossible, filling the universe, pouring down and through, overwhelming. Beneath the cloak of reason rose mindless fear, a chilling wave that subsumed everything that constituted rationality and intelligence. Vertigo followed, the non-world spinning, passing by in an unbearable rush, no beginning, no end.

Space is deep.

The darkness faded, blurring. All movement and starlight flared. There was no warmth to be drawn from the brightness, nothing but cold that could eat through to the soul, cocooning it in ice. The scientific mind could find a loophole in the terror by speculating about this phenomenon, feverishly working to reduce it to a set of statistics. Of course it was cold: out here in vacuum the temperature would barely be above absolute zero.

Space is deep.

That whisper again, seeming to fill the universe. Floating,

turning in this unreality, protected against cold and vacuum. No control, no volition, turning against will. Blue filled the starscape, coalesced, became a glowing blue orb. Far away and then closer in the mind's eye, close enough to see the patterns of mighty winds. Neptune stood against the starscape, blue majesty in the starry bowl of heaven.

This was nightmare, then, not dream; terror rather than release. This was something to be accepted more easily these days, now that time had dulled sensation and numbness was a way of life. The slate had not been erased, but there was no longer a need to feel anything, and that was good.

More movement now, plunging helplessly towards Neptune, drawn in. Again, the scientific mind attempted rescue, considering atmospheric components, wind speeds, planetary mass. The silent stream of facts and figures did not cause the terror to recede this time, and a scream rose, only to be lost in the cold silence of space. A fragmentary rational thought: this was normal, this was the way it should be.

Once again, movement ceased. Painfully blue, rife with the energies of its monstrous winds, Neptune filled the sky. This had become a familiar image, from a time when a hole had been torn in the heavens and lives hurled into it. No sacrifice seemed enough to propitiate this angry god.

There was a dark spot against the blue. Drifting, turning, moving closer now, close enough to make out the outlines of a vessel, sharp and clear, another familiarity in this unfamiliar terrain. Angles formed of titanium, steel, and plastic. Not a small ship, this drifting spacecraft; it had never been intended as a compact craft. A Gothic complexity from end to end, it reflected the passion and strangeness of its designers and builders, the inner world of its primary creator.

The forward motion did not relent now. Closer and closer, then into the metal, into freezing darkness and then into blue light that washed through windows that had no need to be there. There was no gravity, no life-support, the only light coming from the cold brilliance of Neptune. Lights flashed and twinkled bluely all around, moving slowly and gracefully through the air, slivers and splinters of metal, glass, and ice released by some unknown catastrophe. This was the Gravity

Couch Bay, lined with tall glass and steel containers, modern Man's version of Sleeping Beauty's coffin. No one slumbered in those coffins now, nor were any of the myriad instruments operational.

In a dark blur, motion continued. Flashing red scattered the overwhelming blue of Neptune. This was the bridge, crowded with instruments, the air filled with particles of dust and ice. Neptune filled the thick quartz windows, illuminating the corners and crevices. The only relief from the frozen blueness consisted of a single red light, flashing on and off, a bright, bloody interruption, the sigil of an emergency beacon at work.

Other lights flickered now, as though the ship were aware of an intruding presence aboard. Shadows chased around the bridge, vanished again, washed away by the glare.

There was something else here. The lights flickered and cast shadows, but one of those shadows was not stationary. *Floating.*

Space is deep.

Turning without volition, without control. There was a figure at the helm console, hung in the microgravity, tumbling gently. A man, in a flight suit that seemed absurdly rumpled, the sleeves pushed back, indistinct darker spots marring the fabric. The man's arms were flung wide, frozen in place, as though his last act had been to fend something off . . . or, perhaps, to hold on to something that refused to be held in place.

Gracefully, the frozen figure spun around. The man's face blurred from shadow to Neptune's harsh light. He had been perfectly preserved in this environment, of course, that was one detail that could not be overlooked.

The eyes were gone, torn away, the eye sockets somehow blackened, as though by cauterizing. Death had been traumatic and swift, the victim caught and frozen in the act of screaming. Turning, the corpse drifted closer, the face recognizable enough despite the mutilation.

Space is deep.

Plunging back to darkness, and then to gray reality, awake,

sweating, whimpering. Grasping, he found his handhold on reality in the shape of his name: Dr. William Weir, disgraced creator of the lost *Event Horizon*, the stuff of his nightmares.

The name of the eyeless dead.

Chapter One

Dr. William Weir opened his eyes and gazed upon a gray universe. Once more vented into pale reality without argument, vented into a mundane world that was, in its own dreary way, as bad as the world that lived in his dreams.

Lying on his bed, sheets rumpled around his slender body, he stared at the dimly seen ceiling of his studio apartment. This part of awakening had become ritualistic over the years. The ceiling was his icon, his mandala, so lacking in features that he had discovered that it helped him focus. Over the years the ceiling had helped him find his way to one idea after another. Many mornings had been spent lying awake, images and solutions tumbling through his overactive brain while Claire . . .

He turned his head, frowning as beads of sweat trickled into rivulets and found their way into the lines and crags of his face. The dreams took their toll on him, even when he failed to remember anything more than a sense of unease. Once awake he could push the unease, even the terror, to the back of his mind, burying it there beneath facts and figures.

He pushed himself up slightly, enough to reach the bedside

light switch, flicking it with his thumb. The sudden brightness of the halogen light made him squint. The outlines of the apartment came into focus and he winced, trying to deny the sharp jab of pain that always came when he turned on the lights. The pain would pass; it always did.

Framed photographs covered the nightstand, leaving no room for anything but the lamp. His glance over the pictures had become part of his morning ritual as certainly as staring at the ceiling and bringing himself into focus. The pictures were all that he had left, unless he counted the apartment decoration. He had had very little to do with that, unconcerned with the details as long as he was comfortable for the little time he spent there.

There was one more picture on the nightstand, this one unframed. He picked it up, lying back in the bed, ignoring the cold places where he had sweated into the sheets. He stared at the image, trying to place himself there, next to her, next to Claire. She had looked ill when the photograph had been taken, her skin sallow and waxy, aging before her time. She had smiled bravely for the camera despite the way she had felt, despite the depression. She had always been strong, willing to fight her way out of the corners Life sometimes shoved her into.

He closed his eyes, pressing the photograph against his forehead, willing time to turn back, willing things to change, wishing that their lives had turned out differently two years ago, ten years ago, from the beginning.

"I miss you," he whispered, and his shoulders shook.

He put the photograph aside, opened his eyes again. Nothing had changed, nothing ever changed, nothing ever would. The rules of his physical world did not permit such things and would not permit him to turn back time. In his world there was no higher power than the laws of physics.

He pushed the sheet away and eased slowly from the bed, trying to stretch, ignoring the little signs of age in his back, his joints. Denial of the process of aging—more an act of ignoring the physical in favor of the cerebral—had led, for a time, to an obsession with the gradual degradation of his body. That had eventually petered out, leaving him only with

periodic e-mails from the gym about renewing his member-
ship and an occasional pseudo-concerned note from his ho-
meopath.

He walked into the bathroom, habitually making a quarter-
turn to go through the narrow doorway, not bothering to
close the door. A quick leak in slow motion, then a quick
bodywash that sloughed away the traces of sweat along with
any accumulated grime.

He set out his shaving kit, filling a shaving mug with
scalding water. He foamed his face carefully and picked up
the pearl-handled straight razor, opening it out with a slow,
careful movement, reflecting slivers of his lined face. He
turned the razor slightly in his hands, saw the hard, cold
reflection of his eyes.

Dismissing the image, he looked up into his mirror and
applied the edge of the razor to his face, shaving in smooth,
even strokes. This method of shaving was an anachronism,
seen as an affectation, tolerated or ignored by those who
knew of his proclivity. Once upon a time Weir had preferred
it; these days it was no more than habit. Shaving this way
had been another enforcement of precision, another element
in the plan shaping his life. As with so much else in that
plan, it had assumed the air of reflex.

Drip. Startled by the sound, he lifted the razor away from
his face, his breathing stilled for a moment. He clearly heard
the sound of air whispering through the ventilator grill in the
bathroom. *Drip.* He looked to one side of his reflection, focusing on the bathtub tucked into a corner of the tiny bathroom. *Drip.* Slowly, he turned around, staring.

He felt very cold, but knew that the temperature had not
changed.

Water oozed from the faucet, coalescing into a large, un-
gainly bubble of water before giving way to the demands of
gravity. *Odd,* he thought, *that gravity demands so much of
us that when we rest we fall asleep.*

Drip.

He turned back to the mirror and resumed his shaving,
slowly, precisely, and smoothly. He splashed water into his
face, toweled himself dry, throwing the towel over the rack

when he was done. The bathroom needed cleaning, he noted, but he could not be bothered to stoop to the chore often these days. He picked up his comb and swiped carelessly at his hair, pushing it back into place. He was a scientist, and no one really cared how a scientist looked. *Just deliver the super-bomb, Doctor, and we'll overlook your breach of the dress code.*

From the bathroom to the closet, and a change of clothes, half-heartedly smoothing out wrinkles. Dressed, he went into the kitchenette, opened the tiny refrigerator, and stared helplessly into its disorganized interior. New forms of life were being generated in there, he was sure; in the meantime, the examination yielded only the usual archaeological data. One of these days he was going to have to put something fresh in there or arrange for a biohazard team to remove the fridge.

He opened a cabinet, extracted a box of instant oatmeal, added milk powder, water, salt, and too much sugar, irradiating the compound result in the microwave until it was suitably unappetizing and had developed a texture akin to wet, sweetened sawdust. Spooning a mouthful of this unwelcome body fuel into his mouth and chewing morosely, he went to the window. Another mouthful of too-sweet mush, then the last part of the morning ritual.

He reached out and opened the blinds that covered the window. The starscape blazed in at him, giving color to his gray world. The stars were the main attraction in this habitat section of Daylight Station—Earth lay below them, beneath the "south" side, and all that could be seen from his quarters was a cheerful glow at the bottom edge of the window, if you leaned forward in just the right way. Weir never bothered to try and catch the glow, and he never really looked at the starscape, never had, his mind always being on something else. These days his mind was usually empty when he looked out this way, voided in dreams and nightmares. Even so, nothing came to him now, only the hard clarity of too many stars seen through vacuum.

He finished his oatmeal, retracing his steps to the kitchenette, putting the bowl into the dishwasher. Several others, crusted with varying amounts of decaying oatmeal, already occupied the top rack. He closed the machine carefully and poured himself a glass of tepid water.

The videophone buzzed angrily, startling him. He placed his glass on the kitchenette counter, and made his way around to the phone. He could barely remember the last call he had received—no one called him unless they needed something. Most of the people he knew or worked with tried to avoid needing anything from him.

The videophone buzzed again. He tugged at his bottom lip, frowning at the blank-screened instrument. He scanned the nameplate—Microsoft-NYNEX—absently, then, as the third buzz began, waved his hand over the call pickup sensor.

"This is Weir," he said, and was surprised at how dusty and unused his voice sounded. *Take a note, Billy Weir: you need to socialize more.*

The screen lit and cleared. Weir was not surprised at the face that appeared—he could not think of a reason why anyone other than Admiral Hollis' adjutant, Lyle, would be calling him. Station Maintenance, perhaps, but they responded only to service calls, and he had made none of those for a while.

Lyle's face, attractive, dark, too young for the sort of position she held in the ranks of the United States Aerospace Command, gazed at him, guileless, composed. She was making an effort, then, because Lyle never took pains to conceal how tolerant she was when talking to Weir, never let Weir forget how precious every moment of her time was. Lyle sat at the right hand of God. Hollis had never done anything to disabuse his adjutant of this notion.

Composed, smooth, Lyle managed a smile and said, her voice coming tinnily from the videophone speaker, "Dr. Weir, Admiral Hollis would like to see you as soon as possible."

Weir closed his eyes for a moment, blotting out Lyle's face. He knew. Beyond any hope of rational explanation, he *knew.* Hollis should have taught his assistant not to make an effort to hide secrets behind a diplomat's mask.

He opened his eyes, nodded coldly, and waved a hand over the call hangup sensor. *As soon as possible* was no more than MilSpeak for *now*, so to hell with Lyle if the adjutant had a problem with his manners.

He sighed, ran a hand through his untidy hair, and got up to go meet his fate.

Chapter Two

The traverse through Daylight Station could not have been quick enough for Weir. He doubted that it was quick enough for Admiral Hollis either. Hollis was not used to waiting for anything he wanted.

The tube walls blurred by outside the station transport, but Weir, strap-hanging in an empty car, paid them no attention, preferring to spend his time rooting around in the recesses of his mind. He had hoped before, but this time it was certainty, cold and clear, knowledge transmitted to him in the form of a dream. The mechanism was unfamiliar, something he might have rejected without thinking twice before he began to explore ideas that delved into ways of rejecting or reconfiguring the laws of space-time.

He had found a way down the rabbit hole into Wonderland, and he had been encouraged relentlessly, with money, material, and facilities, until everything had gone horribly wrong. Even so, they could not take the truth from him: he had found the rabbit hole and he had shown the way.

The transport disgorged him at his destination in the USAC Command section. People flowed around him, intent on their own business, paying him no heed. No bosun's whistle meaning *boffin on the bridge*, just the odd dismissive look here and there and otherwise blind ignorance. He doubted that many of those in the Command area knew who he was. He glanced down at his security badge once more, making certain it was properly in place. All he needed was some overzealous security thug taking a dislike to him.

He knew his way around in Command, had for years. He glanced up at the wall displays, barely absorbing the images, taking note of the date and time. August 23, 2046. Seven years since . . . There was a cold feeling deep in his gut, as though mercury had pooled there.

He walked slowly into the main reception area. He started to introduce himself, but the unsmiling man at the desk ignored him and stabbed a finger at the vid terminal near his right hand. Weir stood uncertainly in the center of the USAC seal that had, in a flagrant waste of taxpayer's money, been printed into the synthetic-fiber carpet. Symbols and seals and codes by which men lived. So many things to despise, so little time to do anything but sell your soul for a shot at the main chance. The military mindset would not allow a good man to sink completely, but there was always one procedure too many to go through when it came to sorting out the mess.

Weir watched the double doors to Hollis' office, trying not to shuffle his feet while he waited. After a few moments, one of the doors opened and Lyle emerged, walking quickly over to Weir. Lyle was still wearing her diplomatic face, still covering *something*. Weir favored her with an aggravated expression, hoping to give Lyle the impression he was as clueless as Lyle would like.

No more than nods were exchanged before they went into Hollis' office. *At this rate*, Weir thought, *we're going to have a conference in sign language and grunts.*

Hollis' office was still impressive, Weir noted. A video wall, currently blank, took up one side. Other monitors around the room played views of Earth from several different BlackSats. Hollis' desk was a dark monolith sitting to the back of the room, an object even more imposing than the ominous video wall. There was a scattering of equipment on the top, arranged around an impressive black desk lamp that shone with halogen fury. The lights in the office were dimmed down, so that Hollis' lair occupied the most visible spot.

Behind the desk, in the pool of light cast by his desk lamp, sat Admiral John Hollis, looking like a bear considering mayhem. Weir had learned to trust Hollis over time, despite the gruff manner the Admiral cultivated. Unlike many people, Hollis was uninterested in what was good for ensuring the annual appropriation, and had solid notions of what was and was not reasonable in the course of a project. Hollis had been Weir's savior when everything went to hell in a handbasket.

Weir stopped in the center of the office. The USAC seal on the wall glittered with the light from the desk. Lyle passed by Weir and went to stand before the video wall, her hands clasped behind her back, unsmiling, unmoving.

Hollis leaned forward, watching Weir with the air of a concerned uncle. It had been a while since they had seen each other, Weir realized. Hollis' hair had thinned, and he could see deeper lines in the Admiral's face.

Hollis steepled his hands and tried a small smile. "How are you, Bill?" Hollis' voice was gentle, kind.

Automatically, Weir said, "I'm fine." His voice sounded flat, lost in the huge office.

There was a long, uncomfortable pause. Hollis waited, watching Weir, who had nothing more to say and no will or desire to invent small talk to keep his favorite brass hat entertained.

Hollis glanced over at Lyle. Weir noted that the adjutant barely flinched. It was obvious that Lyle could give the Admiral no clues as to the next step.

Hollis looked back at Weir, sighed, and sat back in his chair, idly playing with a pencil. Weir felt a pang of sympathy for the Admiral—there were no easy decisions, no simple approaches to anything. Even so, he wished this meeting was over.

Hollis glanced over at Lyle again, then turned back to Weir. All business now, leaning forward and dropping the pencil on the desk, Hollis said, "I apologize for the short notice, but we've had something come up that requires your immediate attention." The Admiral nodded sharply at his assistant. "Lyle?"

This is it, Weir thought.

Lyle produced a remote, apparently from up her sleeve, gesturing with it. The video wall lit, bathing the office in a faded blue glow that quickly coalesced. The solar system faded up, turned, closed in. Lyle aimed and fired, and the view tilted and accelerated, closing in on the eighth planet. Virtual boundaries surrounded the chosen area, forcing it to grow in size, magnified until the occupants of the office seemed dwarfed.

In the heart of the video wall, confined within a box filled with stars, Neptune shone blue and cold, methane winds re-arranging the patterns of its cloudy surface.

A red dot was blinking in close orbit around the planet.

Stepping away from the video wall and looking intently at Weir, Lyle picked up the thread. "At oh-three-hundred this morning, TDRS picked up an automated navigation beacon broadcasting at two minute intervals in Neptune orbit."

Passing by Hollis' desk, Lyle picked up a sheaf of papers, riffling through them quickly, selecting a small stack to hand to Weir, who went through them hurriedly, going back to confirm the data he had been handed.

"Incredible . . ." Weir muttered. He looked up from the papers, at Lyle, at the video wall, back at the papers, at Hollis. His chest felt hollow, but his heart felt huge and leathery, pounding helplessly in his chest. "These are the same coordinates as before the ship disappeared . . . this, this happened?" He swallowed, hard, trying to force control, trying to grab hold of the scientific approach before his growing excitement started him shaking. "This isn't some kind of hoax?"

Hollis laid his hand flat on his desk, watching Weir now with a flinty, hard look that had a dangerous edge to it. Weir turned his head and saw that Lyle had a nervous look about her now.

"I wouldn't bring you here on a hoax," Hollis said. The

Admiral's hand closed into a fist, and he looked down at it as though it had taken on a life of its own and was becoming a threat to national security. Weir recalled too well that strange and unusual events did not go over too well with Hollis. "Houston confirmed the telemetry and ID codes."

Weir took several steps toward Hollis' desk, then one back, turning to stare at the video wall. "It's the *Event Horizon*," Weir said, trying to get his breath, trying to force his heart to slow down. "She's come back."

Hollis heaved a tremendous sigh, squeezing his eyes shut for a moment, then opening them to stare at Weir. "That ship was lost in deep space, seven years ago. If the *Titanic* sailed into New York Harbor I'd find it more plausible." Hollis paused, waiting to see if Weir had anything to say. The scientist settled for running his fingers through his hair, trying to smooth it into place. "Houston wants Aerospace to send out a search and rescue team, investigate the source of the transmission. If it really is the *Event Horizon*, they'll attempt a salvage."

There was another pause then. Weir turned to look at Lyle, who was watching him intently, then at Hollis. What were they expecting him to say, these military people? This was some kind of foolish game they needed to play, run by arcane rules. As far as he was concerned, Hollis and Lyle could run through their piece, and then they could parlay and get to where they really needed to be.

"We need you to prepare a detailed briefing on the ship's systems for the salvage crew," Hollis said. There it was: *write a report and go away.*

That was not the way it was supposed to work.

Weir turned fully away from the video wall, approaching Hollis' desk. The Admiral sat up straighter, giving Weir a hard look. People could, Weir mused, mistake the Admiral's bulk for flab, not realizing that there was a hard man under that uniform. Hollis was a damn good man, but there were no needless soft edges.

"With respect," Weir said softly, meeting Hollis' eyes, "a written briefing can't possibly anticipate the variables on a mission like this. I have to go with them."

Lyle took a step towards Weir, who turned his head, wary of the young woman. Lyle had a shocked expression, the sort of look that comes when realizing that another person in the room is a dangerous psychotic rather than a simple milquetoast.

"Dr. Weir," Lyle said, her voice harsh, "you have no experience with salvage procedures."

"But I know the ship," Weir said, willing the woman to back down *now*. "You can't send a search-and-rescue team out there alone and expect them to succeed. That would be like . . ." He hesitated, struggling for a simile, running with the first thing that presented itself. He had always been miserable on college debating teams. "Like sending an auto mechanic to work on the shuttle."

Lyle was face to face with him now, determined to make Weir back down and forget this lunatic idea he had that he would hare off into deep space. "I don't see how sending you would improve their chances."

Weir had no intention of giving ground. *His* ship was back. *His* ship. Lyle could not understand that. "I designed that ship." He took a deep breath, staring at Lyle, then at Hollis, then back at Lyle. "I put fourteen years of research into this project. I spent the last seven exploring every possible scenario, trying to discover what went wrong."

Lyle's eyes narrowed. The adjutant seemed convinced that she had victory close at hand. "Your desire to redeem your reputation doesn't factor into this."

Weir had been shoving anger into little corners of his soul for so long that he had been convinced that he could not lose his temper any more. Now, fury starting to burn white-hot inside him, he realized that he had made an incorrect assumption: his anger was only waiting for the right reason.

"This is not about my reputation!" he snapped at Lyle, and for good measure he glared at Hollis. "This is not about me at all!"

He turned back to Lyle, balling his fists, planting his feet. Let them think him belligerent, even dangerous. They *had* to understand. There was too much at stake for everyone.

"The *Event Horizon*," he went on, measuring his words,

speaking as though talking to idiots, "was created for one reason: to go faster than light. Without it, we will never reach new stars, we will never colonize new planets. Mankind's evolution will end *here*." He looked from Lyle to Hollis. Both were watching him, either rapt or guarded or both. "I have to go."

Hollis sighed and sat back, shaking his head. "It's not that simple." He held up a hand as Weir glared angrily at him and started to speak. "Lyle, play the recording for Dr. Weir."

Lyle came back to Hollis' desk, reached down to one of the scattered pieces of equipment. She had the look of a woman with a mission. Weir feared that the mission might well be to make certain that the salvage team traveled unencumbered.

"Navigation Control tried to hail the vessel," Lyle said. She stabbed at a button and looked up at Weir, nodding toward a chair. Weir sat down. "This was the only response."

Waves of sound poured from the office speakers. At first Weir mistook it for amplified white noise, but then he became aware of other things pushing out from the torrent of static: noises that caused him to recoil in his chair, sounds so primal that he had to struggle not to react instinctively. Screeching, chattering voices, barely heard, that chilled him to the bone and sent the hair on his arms and the back of his neck prickling up. He found himself gripping the sides of the chair, his hands locked.

The terrible mixture of sounds suddenly broke, plunging back to nothing more than static. Weir sank back into his chair, limp, shaken by the sounds he had heard. Something in those voices had somehow reached into him, touching the cold parts of his soul.

He shivered, remembering, seeing himself floating, eyeless, on the bridge of the *Event Horizon*.

Lyle shut off the recording. The office was almost silent, only the background noises of Daylight Station being heard. The quiet lasted for a while, none of them daring to speak immediately.

Finally, Lyle politely cleared her throat. She looked pale and drawn now, her mask slipping. "Since the initial transmission there's been no further contact. Just the beacon, every two minutes."

They were doubtless glad for that too, Weir thought. They had heard more than enough with this one transmission. He sat up, focusing. "The crew? Could they still be alive?"

Hollis leaned forward, closer to his desk lamp. The Admiral did not look well. "Someone sent that message."

"Admiral," Weir said, mustering all his strength, all his conviction, "you have to put me on that ship."

Hollis regarded him steadily, the hunter assessing the prey. *I must look like death warmed over.* Weir smiled slightly at the bitter humor of the thought.

Lyle had drifted back into one of the darker corners, deliberately absenting herself from this exchange, avoiding any responsibility for events beyond this moment. Lyle was afraid, he realized, though she might not be able or willing to put that fear into words. Hollis was afraid too, but unwilling to be swayed by the fear.

Hollis pressed his right fist hard down onto his desk, looking down at it as he did so. "It's against my better judgment," he said, and looked up at Weir, "but I'll run this by the Man downstairs. You'll know my decision by the end of the day."

Bullshit, Weir thought, knowing that Hollis had already made the decision and would not need to travel further up the USAC food chain. He managed a slight smile, but his mind was already on the *Event Horizon,* on her return, what they might find when the salvage ship got out to Neptune. There would be important answers out there.

"Thank you, Jack," Weir said softly, rising out of his chair.

"Don't thank me," Hollis said, looking uncomfortable. "I'm not doing you any favors."

Weir nodded, uncertain as to whether he should attempt a parting shot of his own. Deciding against it, he simply turned and, nodding to Lyle as she lurked in the shadows, left, emerging into the too-bright bustle of Command.

His creation had returned.

Everything would soon be well again.

Chapter Three

Hollis watched the door close behind Weir. Then the strength went out of him for a moment, and he slumped in his padded chair. Allowing Weir to go on the mission had not been his preference, considering the shape Weir was in and how he felt about the loss of the *Event Horizon* in the first place.

That's the trouble with women, Hollis thought sourly, glancing down at the pale patch on his left ring finger, *men will go right up to the gates of Hell for them, no questions asked.* Twenty-two years getting one finger indented. A couple of years did little to erase the mark. He felt for Weir. Marks upon the soul could never be erased.

Out of the corner of his eye he saw Lyle sliding forward out of the shadows. Out of the adjutants he had had, Lyle was the smoothest, a slick character who had the marbles of a press agent and the *chutzpah* of a berserker. It was a rare treat to see her unnerved.

Softly, Lyle said, "You're not seriously considering sending him?"

Hollis turned his chair so that he could look directly into

his aide's eyes, a tactic that made the woman flinch. It was a good idea to keep the Young Turks on their toes. "You don't just dismiss Bill Weir," he said, his gruff tone meant to indicate that the listener should expect a miniature lecture. *Here beginneth the lesson, O Daughter.* "The man held Oppenheimer's chair at Princeton."

Hollis paused briefly, wondering whether he should ask if Lyle even knew who J. Robert Oppenheimer was, if she knew the correspondences to Weir's life. *What the hell, it sounds impressive enough.*

"If the *Event Horizon* had worked," Hollis went on, while Lyle stood patiently, her head cocked to one side like a faithful dog, "he would have gone down in history as the greatest mind in physics since Einstein. And we have him here, categorizing stellar objects."

Listening faithfully or not, Lyle was not to be deterred from her course of objections. "The official inquiry blamed Weir's design for the ship's loss."

Hollis slammed a hand down on the desk, making Lyle jump. "That doesn't mean a damn thing." Hollis reined his temper in, calming himself. Never a good idea to blow a fuse in front of junior staff. He continued in a more reasonable tone. "They wanted a scapegoat, and Weir's an easy target. He's not responsible for what happened."

"Does he know that?"

Hollis raised his eyebrows, surprised at the tone of concern in Lyle's voice. "What's on your mind?"

"He doesn't belong on this mission," Lyle said firmly. She did not flinch away from Hollis' unwavering stare. Hollis had to give her credit for her willingness to take a flag officer on in an argument. "Responsible or not, he blames himself. He's too close to it."

Lyle paused and Hollis waited. His aide had yet to conclude the argument. Hollis was not about to make it easier for the adjutant—better for everyone if Lyle got everything shaken out now.

Hollis inclined his head.

Lyle licked her lips, swallowed. "And then there's his wife."

There it was. *God knows we've all wondered about Bill's mental state*, he thought. "It's been two years since she died."

"Some things you don't get over," Lyle said, her tone flat.

Hollis glanced involuntarily at his ring finger. He had to concede that point, if only because some people *were* unlikely to get over certain kinds of emotional trauma. He had seen William Weir on his knees while the gates of Hell swung open before him. Perhaps this was Weir's chance for redemption. The man could use some serious recovery.

"Bill Weir is the best chance we have at recovering the ship," Hollis said, and this time his tone brooked no further argument from Lyle. "He's going. I want our best people on this."

Lyle nodded, moving smoothly back to business at hand, the tension sloughing away like water off a duck's back. "The *Lewis and Clark* just returned from patrol in the asteroid belt. She's docked in Bay Four."

Hollis hated to do this to a hard-worked crew that was due for some downtime and R&R, but he had no choice. If Lyle was pointing to the *Lewis and Clark* rather than an overhauled ship with a rested crew, then there was no other ship within reasonable distance of Daylight Station.

The *Lewis and Clark* had a crack USAC crew, one that was used to the pressure and knew how to take orders. They would deal with it. Hollis could trust their captain to keep them in line.

"Tell Miller to round up his crew," he told Lyle. "They're going back out."

Chapter Four

The hull of the *Lewis and Clark* did a good job of reflecting the state of its crew. The ship was badly in need of a full overhaul, perhaps even a partial refit, after long-haul duty out in the Big Rock Range. Asteroid belt patrol duty offered little in the way of rewards and a great deal in the way of hazards and ship wear.

The *Lewis and Clark* had been peppered with micrometeorites and feathered with dust motes that chewed into the metal as she sailed her way through the gulfs between Mars and Jupiter. She was well known to the Belters, the determined asteroid miners who dug their living out of the rock; for more than a few the *Lewis and Clark* was a lifesaver.

The *Lewis and Clark* was not a pretty ship. Her builders had essentially taken an enormous ion drive and built a spaceship around it, making a place for instrumentation and, grudgingly, for a small crew, a configuration that one British wag had proclaimed to her captain, Miller, as being "All arse and no fore'ead." A muscleship with armor that would make a cockroach cheer, she could stand up to almost anything short of a high-speed encounter with a big chunk of

rock. She could easily deal with a no-maintenance turna-
round and another run, this one taking them much further
than the Big Rock Range.

Inside, she was no great comfort. Captain Miller, poised
loosely in his con as he tried to remain relaxed, looked down
on his demesne. Behind thick quartz windows in the nose,
the bridge was a compacted nightmare of instruments on two
horseshoe levels. Operator's chairs seemed to have been
wedged into the best available positions that might still allow
some movement, suggesting that the human component had
been the last consideration here.

Two of those human components were packed too closely
together at the front of the bridge. There was enough elbow
room, but the feeling on these boats was that you had better
maintain a friendship prayer on a long haul, or someone was
surely going to get mauled, maimed, or murdered.

Starck sat to the left, focused on her navigational readouts,
running cool but intense. She was on this crew because Miller had wanted her on this crew, and he had had enough
clout somewhere to get away with demanding that she be
assigned to the *Lewis and Clark.* Her hair was pulled back,
pinned severely in place, giving her angular face the look of
a professional ascetic.

Smith sat to her right, hunched over his console. Starck
glanced aside at the pilot, who was fluttering his hands over
keypads, laying in their course as he read it from her navigational feed to his console. Where she was slim and sharp,
Smith was somehow blocky, cropped where she was trim,
an abrupt, stiff man. A good pilot, Miller thought, but a lousy
diplomat. Fortunately, Smith's scraps with Belters were few
and far between, and someone usually got in between quickly
enough to prevent anyone from getting damaged.

Suddenly done with his work, Smith straightened, rubbed
at his face, and sat back abruptly, making his pilot's chair
wobble gently on its gimbal mount. He heaved a sigh.

Miller, looking down, sympathized.

Smith tilted his head back, looking up at the Captain's
position. "I can't believe this. I haven't gotten more than
my hand in six weeks, and now *this* shit." Miller saw Starck

purse her lips at Smith's remark. Smith liked to needle the
navigator. "Why not Mars, Captain? Mars has *women*."

Starck looked around and up now, her dark eyes guileless.
"Smith's right." Miller could tell what she was thinking
there: *isn't* that *unusual?* As much as Smith liked to needle
her, she liked to needle right back. "Neptune? There's nothing out there."

"If the shit goes down, we'll be on our own," Smith said.
The pilot had a look of deep concern. Miller could not blame
him for his feelings on the matter either. It was going to be
goddamned lonely out there.

Miller tapped a switch on the main operations panel of his
chair and was swiveled around and lowered into the center
of the bridge. He appreciated the visual effect of this setup,
although he could not see it for himself. He was not a small
man by far; he might have done well if he had pursued foot-
ball seriously, but he had chosen not to give in to the hints
and coercion in high school, preferring instead to pour the
contents of book after book into his brain. The net result of
that was that he could not only strike terror into the hearts
of those he wished to terrify, he knew enough in the way of
psychology and strategy that he could have them running
errands and doing his laundry.

Coming down from the con had the effect of Zeus coming
down from Olympus. Miller cultivated an intense, brooding
look and a watchful air, the image of the dedicated warrior.
He was not a particularly handsome man, but he kept and
carried himself well. Belters tended to appreciate him for his
no-nonsense approach, and a few even welcomed his dark
presence.

As the chair locked in place, Miller said, "You know the
rules. We get the call, we go. Is the course locked in?"

"Locked and cocked," Smith said. The pilot turned back
to his station, his back tensing up. *Does he* ever *relax?* Miller
wondered. One of these days Smith was just going to explode
on the spot.

Starck glanced at her board, then back at Miller. "We're
past the outer marker. We can engage the ion drive whenever
you're ready." Miller liked Starck's intelligence, but had

never gone so far as to express that to her, for fear that she would take offense. Starck had never been particularly approachable.

Miller turned his attention to the other stations in the lower section of the bridge. The boards for the ship's systems and mission stations were down there. Some folks referred to this part of the bridge as "the pit." Miller had never approved of the term, and no one on his crew used it. Such terms tended to generate negative moods, and he wanted as few of those as he could get on long hauls. The crew instead referred to it as the "war room," a term he let slide.

"Justin?"

Justin looked up, eyes shining. "Everything green on my boards, Skipper." He waved a hand over his instruments with a casual air that Miller figured would be gone in another ten years. Justin was fresh-faced still, despite the pallor that the media liked to call Spacer's Tan. At least Justin had some excitement about this mission. Everyone else was bitching about having to pull another long haul.

Neptune. *Better be something awfully important out there.* Justin was waiting, watching him with the eager intentness of a puppy. He took another look at his own boards, then turned back to his bridge crew. "Start the countdown."

There was a bustle of activity. Readouts on several monitors changed to show a digital clock.

Starck said, "Ion drive will engage in"—a pause, while she waited for status lights to change on her boards— "T-minus ten minutes."

"Let's go." Miller released his restraints and rose carefully from his chair. Below him, Justin was rising from his seat, clearing a space. Miller swung around onto the ladder that connected the two bridge sections, covering the distance in a fireman's slide. Smith and Starck followed him down, Smith climbing in that stiff way of his, Starck sliding down.

Miller ducked and turned through the hatch from the war room, his crew following him through the ship, into the main airlock bay. By that time they could have found it by following the sound of something akin to music. There was a jambox at the end of the tunnel, rather than a light, and it was jacked up to earbleed level, making the walls thrum in distressed sympathy with the beat. Along the walls of the bay was a row of extra-vehicular activity suits, stowed neatly, impervious to the pounding rhythm.

Miller came through the hatch looking like angry thunder, his entourage behind him. Before he had even focused on the sole live occupant of the bay, he was snapping, ''Kill it!''

Cooper, tall, black, and bald, barely missed a beat, swinging around and stowing a freshly wrapped safety line in a storage locker. He high-stepped to another storage locker, hitting the power switch on the jambox that had been built into the top. No wonder the damned thing was so loud, Miller thought, as Cooper fell in with the others; the jambox speakers were using half the ship as a resonant chamber.

''Time to play Spam in the can,'' Cooper said, grinning ear-to-ear at his captain's back, his tone sarcastic.

Miller did not waste his time looking back. ''Don't start with me, Coop,'' he snapped, and smiled inwardly as he heard the tone of Cooper's footfalls change. Cooper had smartened up immediately, unconsciously adopting a military posture and gait. Miller was glad he could count on his crew to maintain standards when necessary.

They continued onward to the crew quarters. Everything had been stowed for docking, bunks folded up, chairs and tables put away in their cubbies, the vid units locked down, even the galley cleaned up and cleaned out. They had been restocked for this mission, but had not yet had time to get things into the usual state of a long-haul galley, a situation that was a relief to Miller, who only tolerated the mess because it was particularly bad for morale to be throughly iron-handed. As long as they played the game according to the unwritten rules, cleaning up after themselves every couple of days, he was content to let things slide.

Peters was crouched down at floor level, an access panel pulled up and placed to one side of her while she worked, loading carbon dioxide scrubbers into the ventilation system backup. That had been part of the restocking situation too. When the orders had come down from On High, the maintenance crews had been redirected and all efforts aimed at a fast resupply.

"Captain Miller . . ."

Miller turned his head at the sound of Bill Weir's voice. The scientist was standing to one side of the crew quarters, looking as though he would prefer to be hiding in the head. Miller glared at him, his jaw set.

Weir was not about to be cowed that easily. Staring back at Miller, he tried again. "I just wanted to say—"

"The clock is running, Dr. Weir," Miller said, ice and steel in his voice. He took two steps toward Weir, almost closing the distance, keeping his body language as non-threatening as possible otherwise. Weir tried to flinch back, but had nowhere to go. "If you'll follow the rest of the crew, they'll show you to the gravity tanks."

For a moment, it seemed as though Weir was going to insist on talking to Miller, and never mind the consequences. Finally, he closed his mouth and swallowed hard. The rest of the crew had passed behind Miller by this point, Cooper stopping and half-turning in the hatchway that lead out toward Medical. Miller waited for the inevitable smart-ass comment from Cooper, but it never came; instead, he gave Weir an impatient look.

Weir sidled away from Miller, then turned and followed Cooper out of the crew quarters. Miller stood for a moment, listening to the noises of his ship, the little creaks here and there, the hums, the high-frequency hissing of blank gray monitors. Space was supposed to be silent; spaceships never were. Vibrations traveled from the hull plates, resonated through the ship, manifested as sound from the bulkhead.

Miller turned back to Peters, looking down at her. "What's the holdup?"

"Just loading the last of the CO_2 scrubbers," she said, smoothing her dark hair back. She looked up at him, gave him a smile. Miller relaxed a little. Peters did not seem concerned about anything here, so he saw no reason to worry. Peters had somehow taken on the role of den mother to his crew, giving them a warm presence they could confide in, changing all the rules when it came to the dynamics of crew relationships. She did not affect his authority; instead, she reshaped its effects while providing him wholehearted support. They were a better crew for it, as far as he was concerned. The Belters were crazy about her too.

Peters finished her work and closed the access panel, securing it. She brushed her hands together and stood up, following Miller out of the crew quarters and down to Medical.

Medical was a little more open and spacious than most areas of the ship, if only to allow the ship's doctor some elbowroom. Everything here was modular in format, allowing swift reconfiguration in an emergency. The walls were full of surprises: there was equipment here that major earthside hospitals would go crazy to get. Gravity Couches, tall, broad tubes built for human occupancy, stood against the walls, anchored in the deck plates. Each of them had been opened and activated, waiting only to be filled.

Miller looked around, and found DJ, the ship's doctor, over with Smith, preparing the pilot for his time in the tank. Smith gave DJ an angry look, to no avail. DJ swabbed Smith's arm with an alcohol pad, then, in a flash, jabbed a hypodermic needle into the pilot's arm, pressing the plunger down a bit harder than required. Smith shook DJ's hand off, turned, and climbed into one of the tanks, closing his eyes.

Great bedside manner, DJ, Miller thought. DJ turned, looked for a moment at Miller, nodded, dropped the used hypodermic into a biohazard box, and went on to Cooper. Cooper, as usual, had dispensed with even the smallest display of modesty, standing before his gravity couch with only his sassy attitude and a pair of dog tags to keep him warm. Cooper, grinning, offered his arm to DJ, who did no more than frown, swab, and impale.

To one side of him, Peters kicked off her boots and started to shuck out of her flight suit, going to hang it up in a storage locker. Time was moving; the ion drive would not wait for him. He pulled off his own boots and unzipped his suit, stripping down to his regulation underwear.

Done with Cooper, who went to let it all hang out in his Gravity Couch, DJ moved over to Justin, frowning for a moment at the silver pentacle hanging around Justin's neck with his dog tags. DJ could not raise an objection, however. Just as the dog tags were permissible in the tank, so was religious and matrimonial jewelry. There had been instances of people dying in a Gravity Couch, and woe betide those who thought to deprive them of their comforting icons.

DJ swabbed, stabbed. Justin winced, followed up with a pained smile, went to his tank, and laid down.

"Captain Miller . . ."

Miller turned his head, his expression darkening. Weir was approaching, an almost pleading look on his face. He had stripped down to black bikini underwear.

"Not now," Miller said, sharply. He looked around, found Peters, gestured to her. She walked over. "Peters, show Dr. Weir to his couch, please."

Weir shut his mouth. Peters took the scientist's arm, gently, leading him away from Miller. The Captain was pleased to see that Peters' mothering abilities were effective even on someone as relentlessly single-minded as Weir appeared to be. The last thing he needed was an insistent passenger getting in the way. Weir, unfortunately, had been trying his best to be underfoot since coming aboard at Daylight Station. As far as Miller was concerned, the scientist was nothing more than a nervous, fidgety pain in the ass.

DJ approached, intent on Miller. *Making sure I get the point, as Cooper says.*

Miller offered his arm.

Peters kept her light hold on Weir's arm as she led him over to an unattended Gravity Couch. Weir was not sure whether he should be offended or complimented by this very specific treatment, deciding, in the end, to have little or no reaction at all, blanking everything out as usual.

Weir looked the Gravity Couch over, uncertain. His name was written in black marker on a piece of masking tape stuck to an open area on the operations plate. The tube was lined with padding, the gel feeders almost invisible.

His chest tightened, and he had difficulty breathing. Peters' hand tightened slightly on his arm, reassuring, but it did not make the anxiety attack cease.

She looked at his face, smiling warmly at him as he tried to regain control. "First time in a grav couch?"

Weir swallowed hard, and found that his throat was dry. "Yes."

Peters checked over the Gravity Couch with a practiced eye, inspecting the seals and checking the lining. Taking Weir's arm again, she helped him to get into place inside the tall tube.

Over at the other side of the medical bay, DJ, was administering a shot to Captain Miller. As DJ withdrew the needle, Miller straightened his arm out, flexing the muscles, making the dark skin ripple. Silent, Miller climbed into his Gravity Couch and closed his eyes.

Miller dealt with, DJ came toward Weir, who felt his chest tighten again. Scientist or not, he had been terrified of medical procedures since childhood; needles were the worst. He had never even been able to tolerate local anesthetics for dental work—one look at that hypo of Novocain and he was fleeing for his life.

Distracting himself, Weir said, "Your captain seems to have some sort of problem with me."

Peters smiled again. He liked her smile. Irrationally, it made him feel they could actually be friends. "Don't worry about him," she said, the undertone of her voice suggesting to Weir that she thought Miller was just a big old teddybear under all the gruff authority. "He loves having complete strangers on board."

Very reassuring, Weir thought.

DJ was at his side, now, Peters giving way to him, going off to prepare herself. Silently, focused on his work, DJ took Weir's arm, swabbing it with alcohol. The treatment was not particularly kind, verging on painful. Weir did not feel singled out for special mistreatment, however—even Miller had been handled brusquely.

Still, he disliked the process. Trying to keep his mind of what was to come, he said, "Is that necessary?"

DJ gave him a measured look, not answering for a moment. *Trying to decide if I'm a complete idiot or just blowing smoke*, Weir thought, uneasily.

An eyebrow raised, DJ said, "When the ion drive fires, we'll be taking about thirty gees. Without a tank, the force would liquefy your bones." The doctor's tone was patronizing, and Weir bridled at this.

"I've seen the effect on mice," Weir said, more sharply than he had intended. The ship, he knew, also had inertial dampers that mitigated the effects of acceleration.

DJ shook his head, sighing, and Weir knew that he had failed whatever sort of idiot test DJ had. He closed his eyes and held his breath, wishing himself to some other, kinder, place. Once again, his prayers were not answered. There was a sharp pain in his arm as DJ jabbed a needle into his arm, followed by a worse pain as the doctor injected the medication into him. Weir winced, bit his lip. Liquid warmth spread from the injection site, up and down his arm.

He opened his eyes again, to see DJ disposing of the hypodermic and the swab. The doctor turned back, reaching for the Couch door. He saw Weir's expression, took stock of the scientist's tense posture. "Claustrophobic?"

"Very," Weir said, grateful that someone was at least paying a little attention to him. He was even more grateful for the warm lethargy that was beginning to steal over him.

Unbidden, lines from Coleridge's unfinished "Xanadu" drifted across his mind: *For they on honey-dew hath fed, and drunk the milk of Paradise.*

DJ slammed the Couch door. There was the sound of the door being dogged shut, somewhere in the distance.

Weir faded.

Weir dreamed.

Chapter Five

Fifty-six days out of Daylight Station, with Neptune looming close, the USAC *Lewis and Clark* responded to its
own inner voices. Its crew slept on, entombed in the heart
of the spaceship, but it did not need them, not right now.

For fifty-six days the *Lewis and Clark* had answered only
the call of its own electronic mind. Now it followed a new
compulsion, approaching its target. Maneuvering thrusters
fired in sequence, first correcting pitch and yaw, then, sta-
bility ensured, firing delicate bursts at just the right vectors
to cause its lumbering bulk to slowly roll forward.

Head over heels, the *Lewis and Clark* turned to face back
the way it had come. Thrusters fired again, stopping the roll.
A silent countdown followed.

The ion drive ignited, a brilliance that, out here at least,
shamed the sun. Fusion fire roared silently in the vacuum,
slowing the ship.

Inside the heart of the vessel, another countdown began.
When it was done, the sleepers would awaken.

The *Lewis and Clark* flew on.

Chapter Six

There was a voice, somewhere, calling him.

The world was dark, formless. Somehow, he knew this place. He was a blind man, a deaf man, his senses cut away, leaving him void.

The voice came again, but now it deepened, thickened, became a swirling mass of noise, the massed choir of the damned pouring under and over. Humanity tangled with inhumanity in that terrible knotwork of sound, abrading him as it passed, leaving him bleeding at the edges of his soul.

A tiny corner of his conscious mind informed him that he was enduring the effects of his time in the Gravity Couch. He was reawakening.

Reassured by this thought, he somehow managed to open his eyes, to *see*. The other Gravity Couches came into sight, each of them filled with an inert figure suspended in dark fluid. Fair enough, that was how he must look, then.

With shocking abruptness, his viewpoint whirled about. Suddenly, he was staring at his own tank with its piece of yellowing masking tape stuck to the operations panel. His body was immobile, eyes closed. He could not tell whether he was looking upon a sleeping man or gazing at a corpse. For all he knew, they were all dead.

Whispering again, someone whispering.

The sound resolved slowly: a woman's voice in the distance, voice hushed and bodiless, the sounds of a specter.

Forlorn, that voice, and now it was becoming clearer.

"Billy . . ."

He felt ice creep from his crotch to his heart, and found himself wondering how a ghost could experience sensation. He wanted to explore now, to find the voice, answer its siren call.

Before him, his body, formerly dead, if only in hypersleep, came to life, eyes opening. In a flash, his vision shading to green for a moment, Weir found himself back inside his own flesh, firmly anchored. His world was liquid, warm, filled with tinted blurs. He had no sense of breathing.

He had no sense of panic.

"I'm so cold . . ."

His Gravity Couch drained, the gel sluicing away with remarkable speed. He could move now, if only in slow motion. Lifting a hand, he pressed his palm against the cold door, pushing. The door opened easily.

Another sound in the distance, reverberant in a place that should have been anechoic: *drip . . . drip . . . drip*. The sound of water dripping where it was not supposed to drip.

He looked around, found the crew members still suspended in their tanks. Only he had been awakened and had emerged. *Why is that?* he wondered. No answer was forthcoming, and he discovered that this did not concern him at the moment.

The dripping continued, filling his world.

The voice came again, whispering through the ship. "I'm so cold . . ."

Drawn, he walked, slow-motion, to the hatchway and found that his tentative steps were being made in twenty-league boots, covering great distances through the ship. Within several steps he was at the bridge of the *Lewis and Clark,* standing in the second level, behind the pilot's chair.

Dripping.

Water dripped to the floor of the bridge, making pools, running in rivulets along the plating. The pilot's chair was soaked, streaming. A woman sat in the chair, her too-pale skin drenched, glittering, her sodden hair plastered to her naked back.

As thought rooted to the deck, Weir stood and stared. Uncertainly, he whispered, "Claire?"

There was no answer from the woman in the pilot's chair, nor did she move. She gave no indication that she knew anyone was there.

No indication that she was even alive.

There was only the sound of the water dripping. He could not hear the sound of breathing, not even his.

Slowly, he reached out to touch her shoulder, hesitated, feeling cold stealing over his fingertips.

Fear bubbled darkly within him, rose.

He pulled his hand back, clenching it into a fist.

Whispering, he said her name again. "Claire?"

No movement, no sound, only water.

"I'm sorry," he said, but even this had no effect on the woman sitting before him. "Claire?"

He forced his hand to unclench, straightening the fingers. He reached out slowly, ignoring the cold, touching her hair, feeling the cold wetness. No reaction. He might as well have been touching a statue.

He looked down, hoping for a glimpse of her face, a reflection, finding it in the moribund computer displays. There was something wrong with the reflection, though, something distorted. The planes and contours of her face were shifting, as though something lived under the skin, in the bone, and was pushing angrily to be free.

The fear welled up in a dark torrent now, soul-poisonous and choking.

Panicking, he spun her chair, making it rock on its gimbals.

Claire stared up at him.

"I'm waiting," she said, the sound filling this reality with

undertones of screaming, hissing, crawling voices.
    His soul splintered.
    The darkness swept through him.
    Silence.

Chapter Seven

He fell through the silence, through the darkness, all sensation absent.

His eyes opened, and he was flooded with light. There was a sucking sound too close to his head, then a humming that made him wince, his mind and body too sensitive, too raw to withstand it for very long. There was something in his mouth, coating his tongue, making him salivate uncontrollably.

Surging from the darkness and silence, falling back into the world, he found himself surrounded by metal and plastic, a coffin too tight around him, crushing in, threatening him with suffocation and darkness. There was light, in front of him, but he found that he could not reach it through the wall around his body.

Something moved toward him through the bright blur.

His heart pounded frantically, making the veins in his neck and wrist pulse. Blood seemed replaced with fire, yet he felt cold all over, layered with ice.

Unable to think, to reason out a proper course of action, he lifted his hands and pushed at the door of his Gravity

Couch. The inner surface was slick with the remnants of the gel, smearing as his hands slipped. Furiously, he pounded the heel of his right hand against the unyielding door, trying to make it give way. This effort availed him nothing.

He lurched backward, as far as he could go, intending to kick at the door, to pummel it with his heels to make it give, to allow him freedom to breathe. Before he could strike the first blow, there was a loud hydraulic hiss, deafening in the confined space. His tomb opened to decant him.

Offbalanced, Weir fell forward, his feet sliding in gel on the floor of the tank. With no one to catch him and nothing to grab to stop his fall, he crashed to the deck, his right shoulder, hip, and knee flaring with pain. Gel and saliva poured from his mouth, pooled by his face as he gasped for breath, a human fish drowning in oxygen. His lungs and bronchia flamed, tried to close up, leaving him wheezing and moving weakly as the claustrophobia continued to shake him, closing his mind down in a paroxysm of terror. The medical bay was a vague place to him, perceived through a veil. He fought for focus, but it would not come.

Peters was quickly at his side, one hand on his shoulder, another on his wrist, so familiar, so warm, adjusting so that she could take an ad hoc reading of his pulse.

"Claire . . ." he said, his voice little more than a gasp. The last thing he remembered was Claire. Something *wrong* with Claire.

He felt Peters' hands tighten on him, trying to soothe, trying to calm him back to this reality he had fallen into. He knew that she wanted to get inside his head, to deal with this latest crisis of his, but he refused that help, had always refused that kind of help. He railed against her contact, not wanting to release either the past or the nightmare until he understood it, had mapped the geography of life gone awry.

He gasped in another breath and the fires shot into his head, into his belly.

"DJ!" Peters called, her voice urgent. Her hands tightened again, then relaxed as she said, "It's okay. You're okay. Just breathe." Her face came into view, a curious mixture of mother and professional medic, concerned and observant.

Weir wanted to fight her, to keep struggling for his anguish, but the edges of the nightmare were fading now, and the claustrophobia was easing, here in the open medical bay. There was a sense of relaxation in his chest, and he found that it was becoming easier to breathe. The graying at the edges of his vision began to recede, leaving a scattering of little stars flashing in his vision.

Weir looked up. All of the crew stood in a circle around him, looking down. DJ, emergency pack in hand, was kneeling beside him, checking him over for serious damage. Weir had no doubt that DJ could, if necessary, have him sedated in a matter of moments.

He pawed at the air, trying to push Peters away. She, however, was too practiced, too far ahead of him, and she evaded his telegraphed efforts, maintaining her calming contact. Weir closed his eyes for a moment as his body began to relax.

He looked up at DJ, tried to push himself into at least a sitting position. ''I'm all right now,'' he said, knowing it to be a magnificent lie. Stubbornly, not willing to admit that the truth fell far short of the statement, he repeated his assertion: ''I'm all right.''

To prove the point to those of the crew who doubted this assertion—everyone, as far as he could tell—he tried to push himself to his feet. His legs shook violently as he tried to stand, and his knees buckled, the muscles refusing to have anything to do with his intended course of action. DJ caught him before he could tumble back to the deck, helping him to stay upright. Peters stepped away now, and he found that he missed the contact, the support. DJ was a cold monolith.

''Move slowly,'' DJ said, staring at him without flinching. ''You've been in stasis for fifty-six days. You're going to experience a little disorientation.''

A little. Something dark had crawled into his dreams in the tank, and he was not quite back in the real world now. Reality had not spun around him as confusedly as this since the first time he had ridden to orbit, taking an ill-advised window seat in the big elevator car on Skyhook One. In his experience, perspectives changed enormously and abruptly, following long periods of ennui. During that journey along the length of Skyhook One he had seen his world unfold and refold beneath him, a great blue and white flower afloat in a bottomless sea. By the end of the journey, he had come to an intuitive understanding of the geometry of space-time that had complemented his technical knowledge. He wondered what insights and visions awaited him now.

DJ quickly looked Weir over before letting him go. Weir wobbled for a moment, unsteady and queasy, but finally managed to keep his balance. There was a faint sense of embarrassment at standing there in nothing more than bikini briefs, the center of attention for the entire crew, but there was nothing to be done about that.

At least there was Cooper, still bare-ass naked and utterly free of all concern, leaning in to Weir and saying, "Damn, Dr. Weir, don't scare us like that!" Weir gave him a sickly smile. Cooper seemed, on their short acquaintance, to be Peters' counterpart, a humorous male spirit, a dark Pan. "Coffee?"

"What?" Weir said.

Cooper trotted over to the wall, pulling out a large metal cylinder. He held this up for Weir to see. "Coffee."

Weir frowned in understanding, an expression that made his face hurt. "No, thank you." Cooper shrugged and turned away.

The crew had returned to purposeful movement, leaving Weir standing, confused and disconsolate, in the middle of the room. Miller was already into his flight suit, while Smith, in a corner, did stretching exercises, limbering himself up.

Cooper, still showing no concern about dressing, had opened the metal cylinder and was pouring coffee into a mug he had retrieved from one cubbyhole or another. DJ had stowed his emergency kit and quickly pulled on a flight suit. Starck was climbing into her flight suit, drawing an admiring glance from Cooper who, Weir noted, was mainly admiring Starck's backside.

Without looking around, Starck flipped Cooper the bird. Cooper's eyes lit up as he smiled. "Is that an offer?"

"It is not," was Starck's growled reply.

Weir went in search of his own clothes, trying to understand how anyone could get used to the effects of long-term Gravity Couch suspension. His entire body felt toxic and his mind was sluggish, drained of energy and knowledge. He felt unwilling and unable to accommodate anyone's needs right now—he was not sure that he could even manage to dress.

At least they were close to their—*his*—goal. The *Event Horizon* was waiting, full of truths that were rightfully his. He had sent the *Event Horizon* and her crew down the rabbit hole. Whatever knowledge she had gleaned about Wonderland was his to hold first.

Miller pulled on his boots, quickly lacing them up, then zipped up his flight suit. There was no sign of playfulness about him, only an economy of movement that Weir envied and a fierce energy that left him apprehensive.

Miller turned towards Starck, who was pulling on her boots. "Starck," he barked, "why aren't you on the bridge?"

Starck gave him an acidic look, but it was not enough to make Miller relent. Still, she was not about to be bullied. Lacing up a boot, she growled back, "Do you mind if I get dressed first?"

"Yes I do," Miller said. He bunched his hands into fists, put those on his hips, planted his feet apart, turning his head, surveying his crew, his domain. Weir honestly did not want to cross this man. "Come on, people, let's go!"

Smith was the first one through the exit, followed closely by Starck, Justin, and DJ. Miller turned to follow, then swung back, his face a study in thunder. "And, Coop," the Captain added, giving Cooper's crotch a withering glance, "put some pants on."

Chapter Eight

It seemed to Weir as though activity aboard the *Lewis and Clark*, once begun, never paused for a moment. Miller, Starck, and Smith went forward, into the bridge, to do whatever it was that spaceship bridge crews did at times like these.

Somewhere along the way, Peters had handed him a big warm blanket and he had wrapped himself in this, hoping to combat the shivering. He knew he was suffering from some kind of shock related to the time he had spent suspended in the Gravity Couch, but at the moment he would have preferred not to have any kind of ability to think. Either sleep or a nice warm corner would have done just as well. Neither Peters nor Cooper had been able to convince him that the ship's interior temperature was reasonable—*he* felt cold.

Justin, Cooper, and Peters had set to in the crew's quarters, turning them into a place to spend time, opening bunks, unfolding tables, taking out chairs. The *Lewis and Clark* was a fine example of environmental engineering, Weir thought, with just about everything aboard designed to fit into a niche or fold away. It was easy for the crew to make room or ready the ship for the powerful thrust from the ion drive.

At the moment, DJ was moving around in the cabin, checking radiation badges, apparently for something to do while he avoided talking to Weir. For the moment, Weir found it hard to care—if anything, he would rather be left alone, huddled on a chair at the side of the cabin. This particular misery was not something he had anticipated. Scribbling equations all over reams of paper did not prepare a man for the realities of deep-space travel.

Cooper, Justin, and Peters had finished setting up the crew's quarters and were now comfortable on bunks, Peters watching a video unit. The two men were engaged in pitching a small ball back and forth across the cabin, their expressions gradually easing into mock display of contempt for each other.

Cooper once again snatched the ball out of the air, sneering at Justin. "When are you gonna put some *heat* on that?" He snapped the ball back at Justin.

Justin caught it, staring into Cooper's eyes, challenging. "You can't handle my junk, Papa Bear, don't ask for the heat." The ball sailed back again, straight for Cooper's head.

"Don't play ball in the house," Peters said, not looking up from the video unit she was watching. Both Cooper and Justin ignored this automatic response from her, continuing to toss the ball between them, somehow managing to avoid DJ.

Weir leaned forward, tilting his head, curious about the video she was watching. She had taken out a handheld unit, rather than using the *Lewis and Clark*'s main vid system, and the sounds he had been hearing confirmed his suspicion—this was something of a more private nature rather than a professional production of some kind.

Peters saw Weir looking over at her vid unit, and he had a momentary flash of embarrassment at being caught in his peeping game. Rather than the negative reaction he expected, however, she turned slightly, tilting the unit so that he could see the screen. She turned her attention back to what she was watching.

Weir focused on the screen, blinking as the image changed

rapidly, blurring first with a panning movement, then with a too-fast zoom. He saw the makings of a party, ribbons, balloons, heard the sounds of children and a thin background of music.

The image blurred again, then blanked. The screen cleared to show a child in a wheelchair. Weir estimated the boy's age at four or five, wondering how far off he was. He could make only a bare guess at the nature of the child's handicap, or how long he had been in the wheelchair, though the chair itself did not appear to have been heavily used. The boy was grinning happily, waving his arms. Not quadriplegic then, he thought; a simple paraplegia of some kind, leaving the mind intact and the body more or less functional. Some of these physical dysfunctions could be corrected now, with the help of nanosurgery, but not all.

The boy held up his arms, laughing. "Play horsey, Mommy, play horsey!" he called.

The image shook and shifted and abruptly zoomed back. Peters came into view on the vid screen, looking sunny and relaxed, her clothes bright and loose on her slender frame. To Weir she did not look the slightest bit like someone who spent a great deal of time in space.

Peters, watching, smiled.

Peters, on the screen, laughing, cried, "Want to play horsey, do you?" in a voice that bespoke motherhood and joy. She bent and grasped the child in one long swooping motion that made the boy howl with delight, lifting him out of the wheelchair, flying him through the air, somehow ending up with him on her back.

Somewhere deep inside Weir there was an ache. He chose not to address it, choosing instead to accept the diversion of Miller striding through the hatchway, coming back to the crew quarters from the bridge. He kept his silence as Miller sat down next to Peters, giving her a sympathetic glance.

"I put in for a replacement for you," Miller said, without even glancing at Weir, "but on short notice like this . . ."

He might as well have pointed a finger directly at Weir. Shame burned in Weir's chest, mixed with an uncomfortable rage. *It isn't my fault!* he thought angrily. He had not planned this, and he had not singled out Miller's ship and crew. Miller did not seem to want to approach this rationally.

Peters shrugged and shut off the vid unit, putting it aside. "No, no, it's all right," she said, and gave Weir a friendly, understanding glance, almost speaking to him. "I talked to my ex. He'll keep Denny over Christmas and I'll get him this summer." She gave Miller a brittle smile that told the truth about her dilemma and her feelings. "So everything's all right."

Miller continued to look at her for a few moments, his dark face unreadable. He wanted his scapegoat, Weir thought, his reason for being furious with the world. USAC High Command was too far away, too impersonal, for that purpose. Right or wrong, he had a passenger he could focus on.

Now Peters was trying to take that away from him by not letting Miller use her as a reason to put the screws to his enigmatic guest.

Miller softened momentarily, a flash that was gone as quickly as it came. He glanced quickly at Weir, but there was no challenge there now. He did not expect this ad hoc truce to last.

Starck and Smith arrived, also coming back from the bridge, both of them looking tense, neither of them paying Weir much attention. Starck sat down next to Miller, leaning forward, while Smith took up a position behind the chair Weir was huddling on. Weir looked around, up, for a moment, risking a crick in his neck. Smith looked down at him like the wrath of God, his dark eyes unwavering. It figured, Weir thought. He had managed to usurp the pilot's regular crew quarters chair.

Cooper and Justin paid the psychodrama no attention whatsoever, tossing the ball back and forth.

Behind Weir, Smith intoned, "Two hours to Neptune orbit." The words had all the sound and authority of the Last Trump, meant to make Weir quake.

Smith's pronouncement out of the way, Starck looked at Miller and said, "All boards are green, everything's five by five."

"That's good to know," Miller rumbled. The ball whizzed by him, on its way from Cooper to Justin. Miller gave the younger man an impatient look that was tinged with the suggestion of violence. "Justin, you wanna stow that?"

Justin clutched the ball to his chest, looking abashed. Cooper grinned at him, while Peters offered a "I told you so!" look. Mom might let the boys get away with it, but Dad was home now. . . .

Miller leaned forward, clasping his hands together, his expression deadly serious. "Okay, listen up," he said, looking around at his crew. "As you all know, we have an addition to our crew. Dr. Weir, this is: Starck, my XO; Smith, pilot; Justin, ship's engineer—"

"You can call him Baby Bear," Cooper interrupted, sliding smoothly into the gap that Miller granted him. Justin grinned and Starck snorted, amused.

Miller looked around at Cooper, who was lounging insouciantly on his bunk. "This is Cooper. What the hell do you do on this ship, anyway?"

Cooper gave a show of thinking, his eyebrows working.

Taking his cue, Justin said, "Ballast."

Cooper leaned down over the side of the bunk, threatening to slide off onto the deck. He gave Weir a kissy-face stare that made the scientist flinch back. "I am your best friend," Cooper said, his voice singsong, "I am a lifesaver and a heartbreaker . . ."

Weir was not sure how he should react to this particular display, so he chose to avoid a response altogether. Helplessly, he looked at Miller, who looked impatiently back. "He's a rescue technician. Peters, medical technician, DJ . . ."

"Trauma," DJ said, softly.

So DJ and Peters were the medical tag team, one dealing with the broken ones Peters could not easily fix.

Cooper hauled himself back onto his bunk, his expression serious for once. "All right, everybody knows each other. So what are we doing all the way out here, Skipper?"

"Dr. Weir?" Miller said, turning to look at the bedraggled scientist.

Weir cleared his throat, hesitating. At the beginning he had imagined dramatic pronouncements and grand moments. Instead, he was wrapped in a blanket, stuffed into a spacecraft that had very little to do with human comfort, and presented with a small crew that was almost openly hostile. Had he known how things were to have worked out, he would still have demanded to go with the salvage crew.

It was time he tried to smooth things over.

This in mind, he said, "First of all, I'd like to say how much I appreciate this opportunity—"

Miller rolled his eyes, shook his head, anger radiating off of him in waves. "Dr. Weir," he growled slowly, "we did not volunteer for this mission. We were pulled off leave to be sent to Neptune. It is three billion klicks past even the remotest outpost." Miller took a deep breath. "And the last time the USAC attempted a rescue this far out, we lost both ships. So, please . . . cut to it."

So there was another root cause of Miller's attitude. Rescue and salvage was Miller's life, and he knew the odds for success in most situations. What Weir knew and he believed Miller would eventually learn was that the *Event Horizon* was extraordinary, that the mission they were on was without precedent.

Weir took a deep breath. "Everything I am about to tell you is considered Code Black by the NSA."

Weir paused, letting the crew have time to look at each other. A Code Black classification was not something a crew like this would hear on a regular basis. Interservice rivalries had not waned since the paranoia of the 1950s, with bureaucratic interchanges turning into nightmares of documents, codes, classifications, protocols, and formats. For USAC to accept a National Security Agency Code Black without apparent comment indicated something very serious, very unpleasant.

Whatever was going on here, it was bigger than USAC. The crew had not known that beforehand. Weir wondered if they would develop an increased respect for him. He doubted it.

Cooper looked back at Weir, then at Miller. From his

bunk, Justin said, "That means top secret, Coop."

Cooper looked around at Justin. "You don't need to tell me about Code Black, Baby Bear." Weir heard the attempt at joviality in Cooper's voice. The rescue tech simply could not sustain it.

Weir took a deep breath. The crew was finding its own level for this, giving him a chance to go on. He tugged the blanket more tightly around his body, resisting the urge to shiver. "The USAC intercepted a radio transmission from a decaying orbit around Neptune. The source has been identified as the *Event Horizon.*"

There was dead silence.

Weir waited. He wished he could hide. This was *not* his job.

Her eyes flashing as she turned to glare at him, Starck snapped, "That's impossible!" She looked around the cabin, almost surged forward. "She was lost with all hands, what, seven years ago?"

Justin winced, all playfulness lost. "Yeah, the reactor blew."

"How can we salvage—" Peters started, turning to Weir, a confused expression on her face. He knew what she had to be thinking: there could be *nothing* to salvage, aside from a few bits of radioactive debris.

Standing behind Weir, now leaning closer to him, an angry, threatening presence, Smith growled, "Let the dead rest, man." Weir turned to look at Smith, chills racing up his spine.

Cooper was getting wound up now. Weir turned his attention back to him, hearing him yelling angrily, ". . . Cancel our leave and send us out on some *bullshit* mission!" as he waved his fists in the air. He looked as though he was about to slide down from his bunk to stalk furiously around the crew quarters. Weir did not think that Cooper was about to turn violent, but he was no psychologist. He figured that there was no good reason to put theory to the test in this case.

Miller let the racket go on for a few more moments, then stood up, holding his hands in the air as he bellowed, "*Ev-*

erybody shut up!'' Silence fell again. Weir's ears were ringing. "Let the man speak."

Miller sat down again.

Weir took another deep breath. He hoped that what he was about to say would change the perspective of this crew enough for them to be of use to him in retrieving his ship.

"What was made public about the *Event Horizon*," Weir went on, "that she was a deep-space research vessel, that its reactor went critical, that the ship blew up . . . none of that is true." There was silence now, and he had their undivided attention, having introduced them to the idea of cover-up and conspiracy. That was juicy, something for them to fasten on to. "The *Event Horizon* was the culmination of a secret government project to create a spacecraft capable of faster-than-light flight."

They were all staring at him again, their expressions shocked. This was not something they had heard about, had not even suspected. It had not been possible to keep the *Event Horizon* completely secret once the pure development process was over and the construction process began, but it had been possible to keep a lid on the true nature and purpose of the project. There had been a desire for a deep-space research platform after the successes in exploiting the asteroid belt, and the *Event Horizon* project had played into that, hiding the truth in plain sight. No one had known what might happen.

In the end, no one had known what had happened, out here at Neptune.

Smith, the ominous edge gone from his voice, said, "You can't do that."

"The law of relativity prohibits faster-than-light travel," Starck said, before Weir could answer Smith. These people were still trying to deal with the concepts and ideas illuminated by Einstein; they were unlikely to reach as high as the work of Hawking, or even Gribbin, probably considering quarks to be the noises made by ducks and tachyons as something you used to hang a picture.

Patiently, Weir said, "Relativity, yes." He paused for a moment, trying to bring things a bit closer to the level of those he had to deal with. "We can't *break* the law of relativity, but we can go *around* it. The ship doesn't really move faster than light"—he gestured with his hands, his blanket becoming more precarious with his motion—"it creates a dimensional gateway that allows the ship to instantaneously jump from one point in the universe to another, light years away."

They were all watching intently now, trying to understand him. No matter what, he still felt like an advanced Jungian in a room filled with Freudian novices.

"How?" Starck asked. Her voice had a glassy edge.

Weir shrugged. "Well, it's difficult to . . ." He stopped, feeling helpless as the equations glowed across his mind, a pure blend of mathematics and practical physics. One day he had known how to bend space and had then set out to prove it. "It's all math, you see . . . but . . ." He trailed off again, still trying to reduce the concepts. He had cracked the sky. Now he had to explain it to these people. "In layman's terms, you use a rotating magnetic field to focus a narrow beam of gravitons; these in turn fold space-time consistent with Weyl tensor dynamics until the space-time curvature becomes infinitely large and you have a singularity . . ."

Miller was staring at him, shaking his head. " 'Layman's terms.' "

Weir closed his eyes momentarily, trying to compose himself.

Cooper was lunging over the side of his bunk again. "Fuck 'laymen's terms,' what about English?"

Weir opened his eyes, sighing. How in the name of hell was he supposed to get these concepts across to people who could barely function without an Ezy-Guide and good fortune? He looked around the cramped crew's quarters, spotting the edge of something, a poster, on the inside of an open locker door.

"Let's try this," he said, reaching out without thinking, and tearing the poster down. The name on the locker door, as it bounced shut, was SMITH. That did not matter now.

"Excuse me . . ." Smith started, more shocked at Weir's abrupt action than outraged at his audacity. Weir shot him a look, and the pilot took a step backwards, not saying anything else.

Weir turned back to the other crew members, holding up the poster, making the paper snap in his hands. Doggedly, he said, "Say this paper represents space-time . . ." He slapped the pinup onto the nearest flat surface then made a half-turn, picking up a pen as he did so. He quickly marked an X on the pinup, putting the letter A at one side. "And you want to get from point A *here* to point B *here*." He scribbled another X, this time marked with a B. "Now. What's the shortest distance between two points?"

The crew members stared at him as though he had turned into a raving idiot. What did they expect? There were non-Euclidian geometries involved here, and many human minds could not go around the requisite corners. He knew that his audience resented being thrown back into grade school, but it was the only way he knew how to get even a fraction of the concepts across.

Finally, Justin said, "A straight line." He had a confused look, as though he was certain something was missing from the answer. The other crew members turned to stare at the engineer, who proceeded to glare back at them, annoyed and embarrassed. "What?"

"Wrong," Weir said, trying for a sympathetic smile that he knew was forced and looked uncomfortable. Everyone turned to stare at the scientist again. "The shortest distance between two points is *zero*." He held the poster up, folding it so that the first X was over the second. With a fast, vicious, movement he drove the pen through the layers of paper. Melodramatic but functional; Smith hadn't even complained about the wanton destruction of his pinup.

He lowered the poster, looking at them intently. "That's what the singularity does—it folds space, so that point A and point B coexist in the same space and time. After the ship passes through this gateway, space returns to normal." He handed the punctured poster back to Smith, who took it gingerly, looking at Weir as though the scientist might turn rabid at any moment. "It's called a gravity drive."

Justin was watching Weir intently, genuinely curious. "How do you know all this?"

There was the $64,000 Question. Weir squared his shoulders and said, "I built it."

Cooper made a noise that indicated that he was either impressed or coming to a boil. For good measure, he added, "I can see why they sent you along."

Justin was frowning now, though, obviously putting the bits and pieces of information together and coming up with a result he liked less and less with each passing moment. "So if the ship didn't blow up, what happened?"

"The mission was going perfectly," Weir said, frowning, remembering. "Like a textbook. The ship reached safe distance using conventional thrusters. All the systems looked good." He sat back, his enthusiasm and drive draining as the memories flooded back in. The *Event Horizon* had torn a hole in the heavens and his life had been sucked into it. "All the systems looked good . . . they received the go-ahead to activate the gravity drive and open the gateway to Proxima Centauri, the sun's closest star."

Weir paused for a few moments, lost in the past, replaying those hours, those days in Central Operations. Everything had come crashing down in such a short span of time, taking the foundations of his entire life.

"She vanished from all our scopes. Disappeared without a trace." He paused, looked at Miller. The Captain was watching him intently. "Until now."

Miller grimaced, but his eyes were full of curiosity. He needed to know. "Where has it been the past seven years?"

Weir sat back, his blanket forgotten. "That's what we're here to find out."

Chapter Nine

The bridge was not a place for fast movement, but Weir was managing all right, fitting into a corner. Miller had assumed his throne, of course, but had chosen to sit quietly, listening to all that Weir had to say without spending his energy to comment. So far. It was obvious to Weir that Miller considered his crew to be far more than mere functional appendages.

They had gone as far as possible in the crew quarters, then moved up to the bridge for the second part of the show. If the introduction had rattled the *Lewis and Clark*'s crew, Weir thought, then the next part would freeze their blood.

"We haven't been able to confirm any live contact," Weir said, leaning backwards, his arms crossed over his chest, "but TDRS did receive a single transmission." He felt a little more in control now, a little more together.

He reached out and pressed a key on a nearby computer keypad. The terrifying sound that poured from the bridge speakers had become familiar before leaving Daylight Station, but he could still feel the effects, could still sense the inhuman swirl beneath the static and corruption. Some of the elements rose and fell in a familiar pattern while others seemed to rise and fade in new patterns each time.

Weir watched their faces as the recording played through, watched them become pale and fearful as they endured the voice of the *Event Horizon.* The sounds ceased abruptly, causing them to respond with spasmodic physical movements before anyone could gain control of themselves.

They looked at each other, at Weir.

"What the hell *is* that?" Smith whispered, all of his posturing and his energy drained for the moment. He was staring at Weir like a lost man.

Peters looked up at Miller, who sat impassively in his chair, then back at Weir. "It doesn't sound like anything human," she said, her words coming slowly.

Weir nodded. "Houston has passed the recording through several filters and isolated what appears to be a human voice." It was stretching things somewhat to describe that voice as human, he knew, but it seemed to be the best that anyone could do at the time. There had been no communication from Earth regarding further refinements.

Weir tapped another key. If the first recording had spooked the crew of the *Lewis and Clark*, this one shook them to the core. It was a howl from a soul abandoned and despairing on the far edge of hell. Weir felt it in the darker recesses of his soul even now, having heard it several times.

"Jesus," Smith said. He looked as though the voice had cut straight through him. The other crew members, even Miller, were having a hard time staying put and listening to the playback. DJ had his head down, concentrating.

Miller looked at Weir, intent.

"We're not even sure that it qualifies as language," Weir said, as the playback ended.

DJ looked up at him, his expression dark. "Latin."

Surprised, Weir raised an eyebrow. "Excuse me?"

DJ opened his mouth again, then hesitated for a moment, almost looking inward. "I mean . . ." He took a deep breath. "It sounds like it might be Latin."

Cooper stared at DJ, disbelieving. There was no trace of

his sense of humor now. "Latin? Who the fuck speaks Latin?"

Starck looked around at Cooper, her lip curling. "No one. It's a dead language."

"Mostly dead," DJ said, his voice firm. He stared directly at Weir, who refused to flinch.

Miller leaned forward, looking down at DJ. "Can you translate?"

DJ licked his lips, then said to Weir, "Play that back, please."

Weir tapped the key again, and the voice screamed through the room. This time he tried to focus on the voice, tried to sketch words out of the electronic muck.

"Right there," Weir said, hearing something in the sound. "That sounds like 'liberate me.' " He frowned, losing the thread. "I can't make out the rest. It's too distorted."

Miller leaned forward, now looking at Weir. " 'Liberate me'?"

DJ turned to face Miller. " 'Save me.' "

Cooper turned back to DJ, a dubious expression on his face. "From what?"

Miller sat back, steepling his hands, his eyes on Weir. "You're convinced the crew could still be alive?"

"The *Event Horizon* only had life support for eighteen months," Weir said, considering the possibilities. He had considered just about everything along the way, including the possibility of some kind of time distortion that might have thrown the *Event Horizon* seven years forward. "It seems impossible, but in light of the transmission . . ." He took a deep breath. He had never been able to make the math work for a time distortion. "I have to think that some endured until now."

Cooper looked up at Miller. Some of the playfulness was creeping back into his expressions, his voice. "Skipper, do we get hazard pay for this?"

"You heard the tape, Coop," Miller said. The Captain had a wry expression. "We're looking for *survivors.*"

The bridge was suddenly filled with the sound of a blaring alarm. Miller looked up, consulting readouts.

"Here we go, people," Miller said, his voice gruff. "Stations."

The bridge cleared as Peters, DJ, and Cooper raced back for their standard stations. Weir clambered down the bridge ladder, heading for the flight seat that had been made ready for him.

Strapping himself in, he noted that he was almost excited. He was coming home to *his* ship.

His creation.

He smiled.

Chapter Ten

The *Lewis and Clark* was closing on Neptune.

Miller looked over the Heads-Up Display on the main window, squinting at the bright blue light pouring in through the thick quartz. It was easier to draw the pertinent data from his own readouts, so he turned his attention to those instead.

Starck, also ignoring the HUD, announced, "Crossing the horizon. Optimum approach angle is fourteen degrees."

Miller looked over his instruments and made some quick decisions. Weir could twist space to his heart's content, he thought, but he could never gut-fly a ship like this one. Miller was in his element, no matter how far out they were.

Miller said, "Come around to three-three-four."

Scanning over his displays, he wondered what they were going to find when they met up with the *Event Horizon*. That gut-wrenching racket Weir had played was an indication that *something* strange was going on here. As far as Miller was concerned, second-guessing these situations was a bad idea, sometimes fatal. You could not set expectations and go charging into potentially deadly situations with preconceptions locked into place. You had to be flexible.

Smith said, "Heading three-three-four."

Miller felt the ship shifting. "Make your approach vector negative fourteen degrees."

"One-four degrees," Smith echoed, and Miller felt the ship adjusting course again. *There.* He could feel the thrusters moving to new positions, firing a controlled sequence of bursts that would kill some of their velocity and tighten their orbit. There was something else now—a mild vibration that traveled through the frame of the ship. They were starting to encounter the fringes of Neptune's atmosphere and from here onward the journey could turn into quite a roller coaster ride.

Miller watched his instruments as the *Lewis and Clark* continued its cautious descent. Blue light was replaced by blue-tinged gloom as methane clouds rushed by the bridge windows. The hull temperature was rising as they ploughed into the atmosphere, but the ablative shielding and heat tiles were holding up beautifully, keeping the heat away from the main body of the ship.

Graphic images flashed and scattered across the displays, with one significant image locking into the center of the HUD. Miller scanned this new display with some satisfaction. The information in the display came from the main ID transponder for the *Event Horizon*, and included the ship's registry codes and other identification.

Smith said, "We have a lock on the *Event Horizon's* navigation beacon." He made some quick corrections, focused on his boards. At times like this, Miller would have sworn that Smith somehow fused his mind to the main piloting computer. "It's in the upper ionosphere. We are in for some chop."

Some chop. There were times when Smith displayed a mastery of understatement. "Bring us in tight. Justin, how's my ship?"

Justin was looking from display to display, continually gathering information. He glanced up for a moment, at Miller. "Everything green on my boards, Skipper." He turned back to his boards again as the ship shuddered, buffeted by Neptune's outer atmosphere.

Miller had to wonder how the *Event Horizon* had managed

to stay aloft. As its orbit decayed into the atmosphere, the *Event Horizon* should have been slowed by friction, pulled down by Neptune's gravity and torn apart before the atmospheric pressure crushed the pieces.

Answers. They needed answers.

"Matching speed . . . now," Smith was saying. "Range to target ten thousand meters and closing." The pilot looked up and around at Miller. He had a worried, almost fearful, expression that told Miller that Smith had been asking the same kind of questions about the *Event Horizon*. "Captain, this is . . . this is wrong."

Sympathetically but firmly, Miller said, "We're all on edge, Smith. We're a long way out."

Smith shook his head. Miller could read the tension in the man, watch it ripple under the skin. "That's not it, sir. That ship was built to go faster than light . . . that's just wrong."

Miller did not want to debate the issue or to discuss oddities and fearful symmetries. Smith was making the mistake of thinking things through. At a time like this, it could lead to disaster.

"Keep us slow and steady," Miller said, his voice firm. Listening to him, you might have thought he had not heard Smith.

Smith knew differently. "Yes, sir," he said crisply, turning back to his controls.

Miller turned to Starck. "Starck, get on the horn, see if anyone's listening." He doubted there would be a response, but there were protocols to be followed here.

Starck's fingers flickered over her boards as her eyes took on a slightly unfocused look. "This is U.S. Aerospace command vessel *Lewis and Clark* hailing *Event Horizon*, *Event Horizon*, do you read? This is the *Lewis and Clark* hailing *Event Horizon* . . ."

Miller shut out the sound of Starck's voice as she did the contact mantra. He leaned to the side, looking down in the direction of the extra seat and Bill Weir. Give the scientist credit, the man had not budged from his position since being sent there.

"Dr. Weir!" Miller called. Weir was in the hatchway in

a flash, looking up at Miller with undisguised excitement. It made Miller feel like a fresh steak placed before a starving dinner guest. "I think you want to see this."

Weir clambered up the ladder and onto the flight deck, giving every impression of not noticing the shuddering of the ship as it pushed its way through the fringes of the Neptunian atmosphere. The scientist peered through the thick windows, trying to pick out his ship.

"Where is she?" Weir said. He looked back at Miller, then at Smith.

Without turning, Smith said, "Dead ahead, five thousand meters."

The *Lewis and Clark* shook violently and rolled sideways. Weir grabbed a stanchion and braced his feet. Starck was silent for a moment as Smith's hands flew over the controls.

"We've got some weather," Smith muttered. The ship righted itself but continued to vibrate.

"I noticed," Miller said. He swallowed hard, trying to force his body to relax and quit trying to find a good place to run and hide. Surprises like that were never easy to deal with. They were fine, they were okay, Smith had it under control. "Starck, anybody home?"

Starck looked up, shook her head. "If they are, they're screening their calls."

"Range three thousand meters and closing," Smith said.

Weir was leaning forward, still holding on to the stanchion, peering out through the windows, trying to see past the clouds of methane crystals. "I can't see anything."

Neither could Miller, who was trying the exterior cameras. The weather was thickening out there, as though trying to force them back, or into a change of course. Compounding the visual difficulties, the camera mounts were icing up as the icy clouds struck. The deicing systems were being hard-pressed to keep pace.

"Fifteen hundred meters," Smith said, his voice urgent. "We're getting too close."

Miller looked away from his visual displays, trying to see something through the bridge windows. "Where *is* it?"

Starck went over her instruments, shaking her head,

punched a control, putting an animated graphic up into the HUD. "The scope is lit. It's right in front of us." The graphic flashed confirmation: something there, something big . . .

"One thousand meters," Smith announced. Now his voice held warning. Warning lights flashed red as a shrill beep pulsed through the bridge. The beep vibrated in Miller's teeth and made his ears hurt.

"Proximity warning!" Justin called.

Weir looked back at Miller, then turned back to the window. Miller realized that he had begun to hold his breath, waiting. With an effort, he breathed out, making himself breathe normally.

"Nine hundred, eight hundred meters, seven hundred," Smith was saying, each word harder and harder than the last. "We're right on top of it, sir, we're gonna hit!"

Starck whirled, staring at Miller, waiting for the command to helm that would get them out of there, save their asses.

"Starck—" Miller began.

"It should be right *there*," she said, and turned to point, only to stare in shock as the clouds parted. "My God."

For the first time, Miller saw the *Event Horizon*, enormous and dark as it threatened to blot out the blue of Neptune.

"Reverse thrusters full!" Miller yelled.

Starck and Smith complied.

The *Lewis and Clark* screamed.

Chapter Eleven

The ship bucked and shook, shedding velocity and changing vectors under emergency power. Weir was almost hurled forward, into the windows, but somehow managed to keep his precarious handhold on the bridge. The hull sounded in response to the thrusters, then settled.

The *Event Horizon* was a dark blur as the *Lewis and Clark* shot past it, with no features instantly visible. Miller found himself trying to pick details out, but having no luck.

They came around again, cautiously matching velocity, creeping up slowly. No one spoke. The proximity warning continued to beep.

The *Event Horizon* could easily have swallowed the *Lewis and Clark*, taken it in without anyone noticing it. Weir and his team had created something that was more Gothic monstrosity than spacecraft, a thing of arching girders and strange angles, of darkness and depth that the naked eye and unaided mind could not estimate. The clouds had swirled away around the starship, leaving it at the eye of the storm, but this did not aid in perception.

Miller stared into this darkness and felt cold. He had never felt cold in space before. He let his chair down, unbuckled, stepped onto the deck so that he could go forward.

"There she is," Weir said, pride in his voice. *Daddy's little girl is out there*, Miller thought.

Smith shook his head, his expression unreadable to Miller. "Can we go home now, please?"

Justin had gotten himself into a position to see the *Event Horizon*. He stared for a few moments, his mouth working. Finally, he said, "Jesus, that is one big ugly fat fucker." Miller raised an eyebrow at this uncharacteristic announcement.

"She's not ugly," Weir said. His voice held an angry warning tone, a father protecting his child. Miller was not sure that he liked that tone, but he understood it.

He stepped forward, leaning over Smith like a dark spectral presence. He had had enough of that damned proximity alarm now. He reached down and punched the defeat switch, silencing it.

"Range five hundred meters and holding," Smith said, coming back to business abruptly, a sign of respect for Miller looming over his shoulder. "Turbulence is dropping off."

Starck's fingers were dancing over her board. "Picking up magnetic interference. It's playing hell with the IMUs."

"Switch over to the trackers," Miller said. Starck's fingers flew again, and readouts changed. He turned to look at Smith. "Smith, you up for a flyby?"

"Love to," Smith said, using his least convincing tone of voice.

Smith's hands moved over the controls. The *Lewis and Clark* eased into motion, nudged along by gentle taps of the thrusters. Miller could feel the bursts through his fingers, through his feet, could feel the pulse of the ship and know when there was something wrong.

They came up under the *Event Horizon*, looking into the belly of the beast. Seeing this craft was providing Miller with a different perspective on Bill Weir. He suspected that someone had had the idea to make the ship large and comfortable, a workplace for interstellar crews who might spend a great deal of time researching newly discovered worlds.

To Miller's eyes, the *Event Horizon* was a dark Industrial Revolution monstrosity, the future as envisioned by Stephenson and Brunel, wrought from iron and powered by coal, a foul juggernaut tearing the heavens apart and polluting the remnants with its effluvium. This was not a ship that was easy to knock down.

Smith concentrated on his controls, using the displays where needed, refusing to look at the ship they were passing.

"Look at the size of that thing," Starck muttered.

Weir moved forward, leaning over Smith and Starck, ignoring Smith's warning glare. "Can we move in closer?"

"Any closer and we're gonna need a rubber," Smith growled.

Miller's eyes narrowed. It was time to face the beast. They had a job to do here. "Do it," he said.

Smith frowned angrily. His hands floated over the controls.

Another course change, a bit more abrupt than required. The *Lewis and Clark* drifted in towards the *Event Horizon*, falling into shadow. Miller felt the cold creep into him again, and he wondered what they were getting themselves into here.

Something spherical loomed within the shadows, in the heart of the starship. An arm jutted from the sphere, covered in small pods, dishes and antenna elements.

Weir leaned forward, focusing, pointing. "There's the main airlock. We can dock there."

Miller pulled his attention away from the spherical structure and turned to Smith. "Smith, use the arm and lock us onto that antenna cluster."

Smith nodded. He flicked controls, switching his monitors over to a view from the main camera on the *Lewis and Clark*'s boom arm. Cautiously, he nudged the salvage ship in toward the airlock, killing excess velocity with little blips on the thrusters.

Slipping his right hand into a waldo glove, Smith extended the boom towards the *Event Horizon*. Miller watched over Smith's shoulder, intent on the pilot's work. Weir, in the meantime, was watching out of the main windows, trying to pick out the details.

Floating the arm by the antenna cluster, Smith spread his fingers in the glove. The end of the boom spread open like a flower, the mechanical hand spreading wide. Carefully, Smith floated the hand in towards his target, touched it.

His hand closed in the glove. On the monitor, the mechanical fingers closed around the main part of the antenna cluster, buckling it.

"Be careful," Weir said, turning to Smith. "It's not a load-bearing structure."

Smith slipped his hand from the waldo glove and looked up at Weir, his expression dismissive. "It is now." He turned to Miller, the attitude vanishing. "Locked in, sir."

Miller nodded, turned his head. "Starck, give me a read."

Starck's displays lit, flashed with data, stopping and starting at Starck's tapped-in commands. He liked it a lot when his crew was efficient and smart.

"The reactor's still hot," Starck said, looking over her screens. "We've got several small radiation sources, leaks, probably. Nothing serious."

Miller tried to make sense of the displays himself, but the angle was wrong and all he got was a strained neck muscle. "Do they have pressure?"

Starck nodded. "Affirmative. The hull's intact, but there's no gravity and the thermal units are offline. I'm showing deep cold. The crew couldn't survive unless they were in stasis."

Even then, the odds are lousy, Miller thought. He smoothed at his close-cropped hair, refusing to jump to conclusions until all the evidence was in. "Find 'em, Starck."

"Already on it," Starck said, her fingers moving over her console. "Bio-scan is online." She was silent for a few moments, looking over her displays, mentally organizing the data. Miller expected her to come up with an answer any moment now. Instead, she frowned, uncertain. "Something's wrong with the scan."

Miller leaned further down, trying to take a closer look.

Weir was hanging back, trying once again to stay out of the way. "Radiation interference?" Miller said.

Starck shook her head and bit her lip as she looked over the displays, calling up different readouts. "There's not enough to throw it off. I'm picking up trace life forms, but I can't get a lock on the location."

Miller looked around as Weir took a step toward them. "Could it be the crew? If they were in suspended animation, wouldn't that affect the scan?"

"I'd still get a location," Starck said, turning away from the frustration of her displays, "but these readings, they're all over the ship. It doesn't make any sense."

Miller straightened up, squaring his shoulders. "Okay, we do it the hard way." He looked from Starck to Weir, back to Starck again. "Deck by deck, room by room. Starck, deploy the umbilicus." Miller turned around, found his next target down at the engineering console. "I believe you're up for a walk, Mr. Justin. Go get your bonnet on."

Justin displayed an unseemly level of enthusiasm for this suggestion, snapping back with a crisp, "Yes, sir!" before leaving his station and heading for the hatch.

Weir started to follow Justin off the bridge, hurrying to keep up with the younger man.

"Doctor," Miller said, firmly. Weir stopped and turned, giving Miller an impatient look. "Stay here on the bridge. Once the ship—"

"Captain," Weir interrupted, coming closer to Miller, his face set and his attitude filled with a desire for argument, "I didn't come out here to sit on your bridge. I need to be on that ship."

. Miller took a deep breath, trying to squeeze the tension from muscles that had no desire to be untensed. "Once the ship is secured, we'll bring you on board—"

Sharply, Weir said, "That is unacceptable."

Miller hissed in frustration. "Once we've secured the ship," he said, and now his temper was certainly fraying, "that's the way it is!"

Weir glared at Miller in abject silence. Miller let him have a few breaths to get used to the idea of defeat, then added,

"I need you to guide us from the comm station. *This* is where I need you. Help us to do our job."

Weir breathed out, relaxing. Miller felt relieved. While he expected Weir to be aboard the *Event Horizon* sooner or later, he much preferred it to be later. The last thing they needed was for the main designer of the ship to be stomping around, getting in the way and giving orders no one could follow.

"Very well," Weir said, and he went to sit down.

Miller headed for the hatch.

Chapter Twelve

Down in the airlock bay, Miller watched the monitors while Starck deployed the umbilicus, carefully extending the heavy plastic tube from the *Lewis and Clark* to the *Event Horizon*, locking the docking collar in place over the outer door. At least Weir and his team had done something that followed standard protocols. Miller's crew could have managed without using the umbilicus, but their lives would have been far more complicated.

Miller turned away from the monitors as Cooper, behind him, said, "Come on, Skipper, I already put my shoes on." It was a bit more than his shoes, Miller noted. Cooper was ready to hit space at a moment's notice—all he needed to do was get his helmet in place.

Miller was already fully rigged for EVA, as were Peters and Justin, the bulky suits making it a little difficult for them to move in the airlock bay. Cooper dropped Miller's helmet into place, sealing it securely. Cooper seemed to have an almost infinite capacity for extra-vehicular activity. A liking for EVA was a rare thing even in the Big Rock Range, where being outside was a daily occurrence.

"You've had plenty EVA, Coop," Miller said, his voice muffled by the helmet. "It's Justin's turn. Stay on station. If anything happens . . ."

Cooper was all serious business. "I'll be all over it."

DJ finished checking over Peters and Justin for problems with their suits. He walked over to Miller, checking seams and connectors, confirming the helmet seal.

"Any survivors are gonna be hot," Miller said to DJ.

DJ nodded. "Radiation I can handle." He finished his check of Miller's suit and stepped back. "It's the dead ones I can't fix."

That's all we're probably bringing back for you, Miller thought, turning away from DJ and nodding to Peters.

"Opening inner airlock door," Peters said, doubly muffled through two layers of helmet. She turned and tapped the control panel in the airlock door. There was a resounding clank as the main lock disengaged, allowing the door to slide open.

Miller stepped into the airlock, followed closely by Peters and Justin. Justin turned as he entered the airlock, pulling out the end of a safety line and attaching it to an eyebolt on his suit. Cooper had followed them, still making visual safety checks—one of the reasons Miller respected the man, despite the smart-ass approach to life—and he smiled now at seeing Justin setting up a safety line.

"You still need the rope?" Cooper said to Justin, even as he reached out to check the integrity of the line and its connection to the eyebolt. "I thought you were one of those spacemen with ice in your veins."

Justin tugged on the rope, getting an approving nod from Cooper. "I'd rather be on the rope and not need it," he said, as he tensioned the line a little more, "than need it and not have it. Now step *aside*, old man."

Cooper made a face at this, but confined his revenge to making Justin bend down a little so he could double-check the younger man's helmet seals. In a serious voice, Cooper said, "You just keep your nose clean, Baby Bear. Clear the door."

With a wave, Cooper backed out of the airlock. The door

rolled shut, the locks engaging with a hollow boom that resonated through the ship. Warning lights flicked on. Through his helmet, Miller could hear the low hissing of air being evacuated from the airlock.

He pressed back against the airlock wall, waiting. The seconds ticked away.

Silence around them. The cotton-wool feeling of vacuum, shot through with the sounds of the suit systems, electronics, and electrics warming and cooling, air aspirating through the suit ventilators, odd creaking sounds from the material.

The outer airlock door opened. Light poured in from the umbilicus.

Miller turned and stepped out, launching himself.

Starck had indicated that Weir should follow her down into the lower level of the bridge area. He saw no reason to object to this slight change of environment, so he did as she requested.

Waving him to the seat usually occupied by the engineer, Justin, Starck sat down and started activating monitors and consoles around them. Weir turned his head, taking in the different displays. Three of them were direct video feeds. Time code, and names had been overlaid in the lower right corner; the monitor for Miller's video feed was directly in front of Weir.

At the moment, the feeds showed only the featureless interior of the umbilicus. Once in a while a figure would drift into range.

Next to Weir, Starck said, "Video feed is clear."

Smith climbed down behind them, his eyes on the monitors.

"Are you with us, Dr. Weir?" Miller, made tinny and distant by the radio system.

Something looming up on the monitors now. Weir was beginning to react with excitement as Miller, Peters, and Justin closed on the *Event Horizon*. He should have been with them, but he could not win every battle. Perhaps it was to the good—let the professionals face any initial danger, and then go in to open up all the secrets hidden within the ship.

Weir focused intently on the monitors now. "I'm with you," he said. "You've reached the outer airlock door."

Miller did not waste time with the *Event Horizon*'s outer airlock door, motioning for Justin to get it open in a hurry. Justin quickly complied. Peters pushed by him, then, getting a thumper up against the inner airlock door. The device emitted bursts of sound, measuring the return response.

Peters scanned over the readouts. "We've got pressure," she said, putting the thumper away on her belt.

"Clear and open," Miller said. He and Peters got out of Justin's way.

Justin floated up to the inner airlock door, turning himself carefully. He reached to his utility belt, extracting a slim tool, inserting this into the airlock operations panel. The inner airlock door opened slightly. Particles swirled through the gap—crystals of ice, frozen dust, more that they would have needed additional equipment to identify. Atmosphere from the *Event Horizon* would fill the umbilicus, helping to keep it stable as long as the docking ring seal remained intact.

Justin continued working. The inner airlock door opened all the way, a doorway into pitch darkness.

Justin stowed his tool and checked his line as Miller led the way into the *Event Horizon*. Their helmet lights caught ice crystals whirling in the silent darkness, and light scattered around them, only to be swallowed in the darkness.

Miller glanced around, trying to get some sort of perspective. As far as he could tell, they had stepped into some kind of access corridor, but the corridor was seemingly endless, an immense pool of darkness broken once in a while by a deep blue patch of light that he assumed resulted from windows filtering the light from Neptune.

He looked up. Somewhere far over his head, his helmet light reflected from a ceiling. He could have used a hundred times the candlepower, he realized. The lights they had with them would show them almost nothing.

"Jesus," Peters said, and he looked around at her. "It's huge."

Trying to wrench his mind away from the scale of the

starship, he said, "Ice crystals everywhere. This place is a deep freeze." That was more for Weir's benefit than anyone else's.

Weir's voice was in his head now, courtesy of the suit radio. "You're in the central corridor. It connects the personnel areas to engineering."

Miller was about to suggest they pick a direction when his attention was taken by something hovering just at the edge of his field of vision. "Hold on a second," he said, quietly and firmly. He started to crane his head forward, around. "Everybody hold your position."

Justin and Peters froze where they were. "What is it?" Justin said.

"I don't know," Miller said, edging around, trying not to move too fast. Small objects afloat in microgravity tended to prove all three of Newton's laws of motion. One too-quick move here and they would be chasing this particular mystery down the length of the corridor.

Miller edged down, closer, focusing on the object. It was small and white.

A human tooth, complete with the root.

Shocked, Miller said, "DJ?"

DJ was normally unflappable, but his voice was shaky now. "I, uh, think it's a right, rear molar."

Miller rolled his eyes. Time for the pragmatic voice. "Yeah, thanks, I can *see* it's a tooth." *Yes, DJ,* he thought, *this is not what we were looking for here.*

"Looks like it was pulled out by the root," DJ added helpfully. This was not the sort of statement Miller wanted to have made dead-center in his head. As it was, Miller's spine was chilling, and he could feel the hair rising on his arms.

This was not getting off to a good start. . . .

Come on," Smith said, looking away from the monitors. "What is *that* all about?"

Weir and Starck were both staring at the bizarre image on the monitor displaying Miller's video feed. The tooth floated there lazily in midair, flecked with frozen blood and little bits of flesh.

Weir felt as though he had entered a timeless place, one where the shadows lengthened and the light twisted all the images. His dreams came back to him, haunting. Whatever had happened to the *Event Horizon* seven years ago, it was beginning to seem that the end result was catastrophic and ugly.

Cooper had arrived at the flight deck now, nudging Smith aside as he leaned between Starck and Weir to stare at the monitors. "This is some weird voodoo shit!" the rescue tech exclaimed, shaking his head. Weir looked at Cooper, then turned back to the monitor, wondering what sort of answer he could have given him.

Starck gave Cooper an annoyed glance. "Get back to your post, Cooper."

Weir wondered whether it mattered if Cooper spent his time here on the bridge or down in the airlock bay playing doorman. Cooper did not stick around to debate the point, leaving the bridge after a curt nod to Starck.

The image on Miller's monitor shifted.

Miller stood up straight, stretching his arms out, the motion sending the vagrant tooth spinning away down the corridor. This mission was beginning to give him the creeps, and that was just not acceptable.

"All right, all right," he said, pushing his feelings aside and trying to regain his professional demeanor, "let's move on. Peters and I will search the forward decks." He turned to look at Justin, who was trying to follow the progress of the flying tooth. "Justin, take engineering. Don't forget to breathe."

Justin turned his head. Miller could just about see him smiling through the faceplate. "I won't, sir."

Miller and Peters started cautiously down the corridor. If Miller had his bearings right, they would eventually arrive at the bridge. In contrast, Justin tackled the travel issue by kicking off hard, aiming for a wall, turning over in midflight, and kicking off from there to increase his momentum. He vanished down the corridor, trailing line.

Miller shook his head, smiling. Justin was good, but he was young and sometimes impetuous.

He passed through an archway, surprised at the suggestion of Gothic design here. It took him a moment to realize that the archway disguised a join in the corridor—sections of the main corridor had been joined together this way, rather than simply being welded or bolted. He stopped and turned carefully, inspecting the coupling.

Near the floor, a box caught his attention. There was an explosives symbol on the cover.

"Dr. Weir," Miller said, slowly, "what's this?"

Before Weir could answer, Peters said, "Here's another one." She was at another coupling, hovering over another of the boxes. She pointed towards the other side of the corridor. "They're all over the place."

Looking around, Miller could pick out those within range of his helmet light. They nestled into the couplings at floor or ceiling level, looking for all the world like mechanical molluscs.

"They're explosive charges," Weir said, finally.

Miller sighed, shaking his head. "I can see that. What are they for?"

"In an emergency, they destroy the central corridor and separate the personnel areas from engineering. The crew could use the foredecks as a lifeboat."

This made sense to Miller, though he had some difficulty seeing it from an aesthetic point of view—all this immensity, this grandeur, and the panic button led to a collection of explosives out in the open. The *Event Horizon* had been the prototype. Not everything gets covered up in a prototype.

Miller joined Peters and they began moving down the corridor again. "That means they didn't abandon ship," Peters said.

Miller was looking around again, trying to figure out what was *really* wrong here. "So where are they?" he asked.

No answers were forthcoming.

Chapter Thirteen

Weir scanned the monitors with an almost boyish enthusiasm, concentrating mainly on the feeds from Miller and Peters—right now, Justin's progress was more dizzying than informative.

Miller and Peters had reached the *Event Horizon*'s Gravity Couch Bay. This would be one of the places they would find any crew members in suspended animation. Against all reason, Weir held out hope that they would find someone alive.

Peters said, "We found the Gravity Couches." The radio link made her voice tinny.

There were eighteen Couches in the bay, nine on each of the two walls, all essentially the same in form, size, and function as those on the *Lewis and Clark*. The bay itself was considerably larger, of course, but everything aboard the *Event Horizon* was designed to be on the large side.

"Any crew?" Weir said, as Peters and Miller each walked along a row of Gravity Couches.

"Negative," Miller said.

Weir sat back, drained, empty. It was hopeless, then. No one left alive, no easy route to the answers. They *had* to know. There must be something aboard the ship. . . .

The video monitor showed nothing but one empty Gravity Couch after another. They gave no sign of having been used. Weir shook his head, trying to will something into being there.

"They're empty, Dr. Weir," Miller said.

Weir's fists clenched. *Hopeless.* Everything he had done ended up in a condition of hopelessness. He looked up, looked into the darkness of the *Event Horizon* and tried to think of Claire, but he could not get the focus now, could not bring her back to mind.

"Starck," Miller continued, "any luck with that scan?"

Starck's hands were playing over the console in front of her. Weir turned his head to look at her and saw frustration written in lines and knots in her face.

"I'm running diagnostics now, Captain." She shook her head again, glaring at the readouts. "Nothing's wrong with the sensor pack. I'm still getting trace life readings all over the ship."

That should have been impossible, Weir reflected. Miller knew that too, going by the tinny sigh over the radio link.

A change in the frantic movement on Justin's monitor drew Weir's attention away from Starck's predicament. Justin had given up his fastball flying technique now, in favor of more considered movement. As Weir watched, the image from Justin's camera stabilized and focused. Weir smiled, though it was an empty smile. Justin was about to encounter one of the truths of the *Event Horizon*.

Justin stood before an immense dark door, perhaps the biggest pressure door he had ever seen in his life. Despite himself, he was extremely impressed. If he had believed in such books of mythology, he might even have found something biblical about it.

As it was, it was big. Goddamned big. Huge, in fact.

Cheerfully, he said, "I've reached the First Containment door."

"The engineering decks are on the other side," Weir answered. Justin felt a flash of annoyance at the scientist. Weir might be one of the most brilliant minds ever to juggle an equation, but he was surely one condescending sonofabitch when he felt like it.

Justin did not bother to acknowledge Weir's statement. He reached out and touched the access panel at his right hand side. The door opened with ponderous grace.

Justin was delighted to see yet more mystery revealed behind this First Containment door. He moved forward to see more clearly, and to give his camera a better chance to pick up what he was seeing. He was looking into a long corridor section, tube-shaped. The engineers who had built the ship had, for some arcane reason, set this section of corridor to spinning like a turbine, a shell outside the access tube whirling at dizzying speed. From Justin's vantage point, it looked as though alternating sections were spinning in different directions. There was surprisingly little noise, but he figured most of it operated in vacuum to cut down on friction.

His head spun as he tried to focus on this weird assembly. Finally, he looked away, trying to get his bearings back. "Cool," he said. "What's all this do?"

Weir said, "It allows you to enter the Second Containment without compromising the magnetic fields."

Okay, so you're into big showy rigs. Justin suspected that the same result could have been achieved with half the equipment and a quarter of the power, but he wasn't the one who had the brain the size of Betelgeuse.

"Looks like a meatgrinder," he said, and stepped forward, his breath echoing in his helmet.

Dr. Weir, what's this door?" Peters asked.

She had continued all the way down the main corridor until the corridor had ended in a pressure door. She played her helmet light over it, over the walls and floor nearby. Nothing to be seen.

"You're at the bridge, Ms. Peters," Weir said over the radio link.

She took a deep breath and started to reach for the door controls.

*   *   *

Miller passed through a hatchway into what appeared to be some kind of medical facility, either the operating theater or some kind of surgical lab. All of the tables were empty, reflecting his helmet light, and as he turned his head he caught glimpses of surgical instruments and equipment floating aimlessly in the microgravity.

"I'm in Medical," he said, ducking out of the way of a wandering forceps. He continued his exploration, moving cautiously through the room, inspecting everything. "No casualties. It looks like this place hasn't been used."

Secured drug lockers, empty biohazard and sharps containers, just an ugly assortment of floating hardware to contend with. Miller's skin was crawling with cold. He was beginning to think Smith was right, that they should not have come here.

Over the radio link, Weir said, "You still haven't seen any crew?"

"If we saw any crew, Doctor, you'd know about it." He turned his head, looked down at the floor, looking for clues and coming up with nothing. Under his breath he muttered, "This place is a tomb."

He took a step forward.

Someone tapped him on the shoulder.

"Fuck!" Miller yelled, whirling, his hands coming up, ready to strike out.

An empty glove drifted past his faceplate, tumbling slowly. He stared at it as it floated away. His heart was thundering in his chest and his breathing was roaring in his ears.

"Miller?" Starck was demanding over the radio link. "You okay?"

"I'm fine," he said, the words coming as a reflex. He slowed his breathing, tried to get his heart to slow down to a more normal rate. He could feel the clamminess of sweat on his skin, cooled by the air circulating through his suit.

"Your pulse is elevated," DJ said over the radio link. "Are you sure you're—"

"*I'm fine,*" Miller snapped, which put a stop to any further questions from DJ.

He turned, pushing the fright to the back of his mind. Only

inanimate objects, nothing more. Finding a computer console, he set to work. He had had enough of fishing around in the dark. They needed light, air, warmth.

He settled in to start hacking into the ship's systems.

Weir hunched over in his seat, his hands clenched into fists. He stared at the monitors, but nothing new was revealed.

"Where are they?" he whispered.

Starck turned to him, her face set. "If anyone's there to be saved, Miller's going to save them. No one's got more hands-on experience in this. He's one of the few captains who've ever worked the Outer Reach."

That got Weir's attention for the moment. "He's been past Mars?"

Starck turned her head, checking displays. "He served on the *Goliath.*"

Weir shuffled information in his mind. "The *Goliath?* Wasn't that ship destroyed in a fire?"

"They were trying to rescue a supply shuttle bound for Titan," Starck said, slowly. "The freighter's tanks ruptured, flooded both ships with pure oxygen." That was one of the great spacer nightmares: a ship filled with oxygen was a deathtrap about to happen. "Miller and three others barely made it to a lifeboat. If not for Miller, no one would have made it."

Weir gazed at her, thoughtful. Miller was strong, then, resourceful. That was good.

Wasn't it?

Peters had managed to open the hatch to the bridge. Taking a deep breath, she eased inside, glancing quickly around.

"Okay," she said, "I'm on the bridge."

She moved slowly around, finding a briefing table and several chairs. This was an antechamber to the bridge, a small briefing room that the crew would have used for mission discussions and assignments. She looked over the table and chairs but found no indication that they had ever been used.

There was a brilliant flash of lightning, storm activity going on in the atmosphere of the planet beneath them. She started to look up, but the flash had thrown off her night vision for a few moments.

She turned to move deeper into the bridge, leaving behind, high up on a wall, unnoticed, a frozen mass of blood and tissue that had once been a living human being.

Miller worked at the science station for a couple of minutes, and was suddenly rewarded by displays lighting up. He smiled to himself. Something was finally going the way he wanted it. This was something he could deal with.

Pausing for a moment, he said, "The science workstation has power. I'll see if I can find the crew from here."

He got back to work.

We're not going to find anyone," Smith said to Starck, his face an angry mask. "This place is dead."

Weir ignored him, ignored Miller's monitor and Justin's continuing walk into engineering. He was staring at Peters' monitor now, reading the details of the bridge as best he could. They needed to restore power to the *Event Horizon* as quickly as possible.

"Ms. Peters," Weir said softly, "turn back and to your left, please."

He watched as Peters' camera view moved, bringing something new into view.

Starck leaned over, peering at the monitor, then at Weir. "What is it?"

"Ship's log," Weir said.

"I see it," Peters said, and the view on her monitor shifted again.

Peters stepped toward the log unit. It was really nothing more than a small videodisc unit built into one of the consoles, but it was enough to keep a running record of bridge and ship activities.

She reached down and pressed the eject tab. Nothing happened. She leaned down, checked that it was receiving power. A small green light was glowing in one corner of the operations panel. She tried the eject button again, without success.

"It's stuck," she said.

She reached down to her utility belt, extracting a small probe. Carefully, she slipped the probe into the video unit, feeling around until she was sure she had the eject mechanism. She pressed down, pulled back, felt something give.

A tiny laserdisc emerged halfway from the unit, jamming there. Peters grasped it carefully and pulled, but the disc would not move any further. She tugged again, frustrating herself in the effort.

"It's really jammed in there," she said.

She sighed, then growled softly. They needed that disc, needed it badly. It might well answer a lot of the questions about the fate of the crew. It might even answer some of the questions about the disappearance of the *Event Horizon*. All things considered, she would be glad to see Weir's mind put at ease.

She tried the probe again, trying to pull the laserdisc away from whatever part of the mechanism was jamming it in place. This did not seem to help. Once again she grasped the disc and pulled, was frustrated, tugged harder, thought she had it this time, but didn't.

All the air rushing out of her in one explosive gasp, she put all of her strength into getting the disc loose. This time it came free, sending her spinning and tumbling in the microgravity.

She flung an arm out, trying to stabilize herself long enough to get back to a position where she might be able to stop her motion. Her heart leapt into her mouth as her helmet lights flashed on something floating in the bridge with her.

She turned helplessly, only to find herself being struck by something with considerable mass. Holding on to the laserdisc with her right hand, she reached out with her left, grasping cloth and, beneath that, something hard.

A face came into view, lit brightly by her helmet lamps. A man's face, contorted, mouth open, swollen tongue protruding. The veins stood out, bloated and frozen, all over his face and neck.

She stared for a moment, her breath catching in her throat. She pushed away from the body, rebounded from a wall, managed to bounce herself down to the deck, catching hold of the edge of a console to stop herself from moving any further.

Her tone utterly professional, she said, "I found one." Her heart was pounding, but it did not feel as though she was in any danger of her control slipping. Good enough.

Over the radio link, Miller said, "Alive?"

"Corpsicle," she said.

She lifted her head, aiming her lights up at the floating corpse. Anchoring herself against one of the console units, she reached up, snagging the corpse by a foot, pulling it down.

Weir sat back now, regarding the face of the dead man on Peters' monitor. Whoever he was, he was a mess, and they'd be lucky to identify him easily.

DJ came into the bridge, joining Weir and Starck at the monitors.

"What happened to his eyes?" Smith said, staring at the screen.

"Explosive decompression," Starck said.

DJ shook his head. "Decompression wouldn't do that."

Weir had to agree there. The dead man's eyes had been gouged out, going by the images.

That would have to wait for the time being. Justin had finished his long walk.

Chapter Fourteen

Justin walked slowly out of the spinning tube, his head filled with an annoying buzz that he knew he would not be rid of for some time. He looked around, finding himself in some kind of operational alcove that opened out into a huge spherical chamber.

It was not easy to see anything. His helmet light reflected from a gray slick that seemed to coat everything in the alcove. He had only a moment to try and figure out which way to turn before something wet and massy struck his suit. Liquid gray shot up in front of his faceplate, out in front of his hands, splashing over his fingers. Other floating globules of liquid caught the light from his helmet.

Then his light was gone, coated by the same thick gray fluid as a another globule struck his helmet.

He reached up, trying to clear the stuff from his helmet. He managed to get some of his light back, but it was very little help. This was already trouble, and not likely to get much better if he stayed in here.

For the benefit of those on the bridge, he said, "I'm in the Second Containment. There must have been a coolant leak.'' He wiped at his faceplate and helmet lights again. Looking around, he was able to get an idea of just how much of the gray stuff was actually hanging in the air. Fluid in microgravity was a menace. ''Man, this shit is everywhere. I can't see a damn thing.''

That wasn't quite true. There was a console nearby, facing out into the larger chamber. He could see some dim lights on the board, beneath the muck. He floated himself over to it, batting balls of coolant out of the way, mainly causing them to become smaller balls of coolant. Grabbing the edge of the console with one hand, he hauled himself down, anchoring himself as best he could while he used one glove to wipe coolant away from the console. He tried not to think about the radiation level.

His attempt at cleanup yielded good results. The board was alive and functional, operating in standby mode. He tapped keypads and was rewarded by the appearance of a variety of readouts.

''The reactor's still hot,'' he said, putting pieces together as he gathered data from the console. ''Coolant level is on reserve, but within the safe-line.''

He tapped in more commands.

The lights came up abruptly, almost blinding him. ''I did it!'' he crowed, feeling pleased with himself for a moment.

The air was thick with lead-gray balls of coolant. He looked around, finding that the viscous fluid had indeed coated just about every surface.

He turned his attention away from the control area and looked out towards the larger chamber. That chamber had lit up too, lights coming on at all angles.

Justin stood and stared for a few moments, his mouth hanging open in awe. He had expected a large open area here, but this was off the scale. There were baseball stadiums smaller than the Second Containment. The curving walls rose for dozens of meters overhead, sank for dozens of meters below, a rippling darkness studded with the spiky forms of control rods.

''Holy shit,'' Justin said, trying to take it all in.

At the center of the Second Containment, as black as midnight, was an unholy-looking construction. Justin estimated it to be at least ten meters in diameter, perhaps larger, a broad torus covered on the outside by a series of spikes, occupied on the inside by a huge dark sphere that resembled nothing more than a rotted, mottled orange. Trying to make sense of the construction, Justin felt his sense of perspective being twisted around. He felt faintly sick.

Parts of the device seemed to be moving, shifting, the surfaces slick and oily. He had the feeling that there was enormous power here. Time and space were under siege.

His gut clenched.

"Justin?" It was Cooper. The voice jolted him back into place, letting him grasp his professional state of mind.

"I think I found something," he said.

He could not stop staring.

Starck, Weir, and Smith were huddled around the monitor carrying Justin's video feed. For a while the images had been smeary, thanks to the coolant, but Justin had managed to remove most of it, clearing the image up considerably. The addition of decent amounts of light had helped.

Weir felt relaxed. The *Event Horizon* was not in the best shape, but it was still flightworthy, perhaps even capable of carrying out its intended function of warp flight.

"What *is* that?" Starck asked, pointing at the construction in the middle of the screen. It was tricky to watch—even seen through a relatively poor vid feed, the device seemed to shift and twist, playing hell with rational perspective.

Weir sat forward, not bothering to hide the pleasure he felt in his creation. "That's the Core—the gravity drive. The heart of the ship."

Smith turned to look at Weir. "You built that?"

"Yes."

Smith was silent for a long moment, watching Weir. "You didn't have a very happy childhood, did you?"

Justin eased past the main console, and down onto the gantry that led out into the center of the Second Containment. From this point of view, the containment unit was even more im-

pressive, even if it did feel a little like being on the inside
of the universe's biggest Iron Maiden.

He looked upward, having to strain to do so, seeing lights
overhead that appeared to be barely more than twinkles in
the night. He had to wonder at the design ethic behind all of
this—Weir and his team had to have lived by night alone to
have created something as grim as this section.

He did not want to consider what it took to create something like the strangeness lurking in the heart of this darkness. The human mind was not meant to go around such
corners, even if the corporeal form could make the journey.
He was used to the notion of crossing between the worlds,
but this was a doorway it would be safer not to go through.

He closed on the construction, focusing on the sphere inside the torus. Something rippled across the surface, vanished, rippled again. The last thing they needed now was for
this thing to crack open and spill itself all over the ship.

"I think I see something," he said, and reached down to
his belt, pulling out a tool, a sensor unit that would give him
a better idea as to whether or not there was a rupture in the
Core.

He leaned in toward the Core.

Starck jerked back, startled as Justin's monitor went to static.
The radio link hissed like a snakepit for a moment, before
the filters cut in and squelched the racket.

"Hold on a sec," Starck said. She did something with the
console, but Weir could not get a clear view. "You're breaking up."

The monitor cleared for a moment, then static took it
again. Starck gave Weir a worried look.

Justin activated the sensor unit, trying to maintain his position as he pushed it out toward the Core.

There was a hiss of static in his earphones, then Starck's
voice breaking through for a moment ". . . Justin . . . ?" Her
voice vanished again.

His helmet light flickered off, on, dimmed down. He hesitated for a moment, wondering if he should deal with it

before going on. Probably just a result of the coolant splashing into his helmet, either the lamp terminals or the battery unit getting crocked by the flying sludge.

He reached up and tapped the lamp.

Justin, come in,'' Starck was repeating. Weir sat silently now, watching her, while Smith leaned down between them, his face ashen.

There was a beep from the console next to Starck, startling Weir. Starck looked around. The bio-scan display, frustrating in its quiescence until now, was displaying readings into the red sector of the scale.

· Something was awry, Weir thought. Then again, something had been awry with this mission since they had located the *Event Horizon*.

"What is it?" Weir said.

Starck shook her head, going over the displays. "I don't know. The life readings just went off the scale."

"Something's wrong," Smith said, his voice forceful. Weir almost spoke up in agreement, but chose to remain silent instead. "Pull them out."

Starck looked at Weir.

Weir said nothing.

Justin's monitor flared with static.

Justin pressed the sensor unit up against the side of the spherical unit. He had expected it to be a firm contact, but the surface felt soft, spongy, almost as though it was composed of some kind of organic material.

The shifting sensation stopped.

Justin looked up from the sensor.

In front of him, the Core darkened, somehow taking on the color of nothingness. All around, the containment unit seemed to be sharper, clearer, as though everything around him had focused, revealing incredible amounts of detail. Even the arm of his suit, the hand held out with the pressure sensor against the Core, had an unreal clarity.

Justin was aware of light. There was no sound.

Then the power, a force beyond reckoning that reached

around him, intruded into his universe, enveloping him without pause for consent or complaint.

The void rose up around him, embracing.

Unresisting, Justin fell into the space between the worlds and was gone.

Reality began to tremble around the Core.

Chapter Fifteen

Cooper was not in the mood for this, not in the slightest. *Baby Bear, you'd better be kidding me....*

Justin's safety line was unreeling at an insane, impossible rate. Cooper had tracked the line usage from the start, watched it pay out fast and slow.

Now it was paying out at a rate the counter had problems tracking.

"Three-fifty meters, four hundred meters," he read off. He grabbed his helmet, got it on, the adrenaline starting to pump now. Justin was in trouble.

DJ helped Cooper seal the helmet down. A quick suit check, a thumbs-up.

"I'm gone!" Cooper yelled, slapping the control to open the inner airlock door. His heart was pounding and he felt crazy. He hated this more than anything. When it was over, all he would want to do was throw up and shake. Right now there was no time to think.

The inner airlock door closed behind him. The outer door hissed open. Shutting his mind off, he dove into the umbilicus.

Hold on, Baby Bear, he thought frantically, *Papa Bear's coming to get you.*

Like a nightmare, the *Event Horizon* loomed up ahead of him.

He plunged into the airlock.

Chapter Sixteen

Darkness rolled out, folded in upon itself.

The safety line going into the Core tightened, then rippled, as though refracted through water.

Space contracted, expanded.

Reality warped, a wave traveling silently out from the Core. Light bent.

The wave passed through the Second Containment walls as though they were air.

Swept into the antechamber, pushing coolant away and into the walls, the console. Debris erupted, slammed into walls, floor, ceiling, ricocheted away as the wave passed.

Swept outward, down the main corridor. Windows vibrated as it passed.

The safety line tightened again, sang, twanged, relaxed.

Cooper shot down the corridor. The wave caught him in midair, spun him, sent him flat against the wall, swearing, the wind knocked out of him for a moment as he caromed away toward the opposite wall. He managed to roll before he hit, hitting the wall feet-first, kicking off again.

The wave ripped down the main corridor. Debris swirled

before it, flotsam that had been equipment or component parts of human beings.

The *Event Horizon* was beginning to resonate now, the superstructure sounding with a deepening roar that suggested that the ship was about to tear apart.

The hatchway to the medical bay slammed open, the door buckling and a hinge tearing. A wave of medical debris swirled up before the wave.

Miller grabbed the edge of the computer station he had been working on, ducking as debris pelted him. The wave pulled him up from his haven, wrenched him away from the console, and slammed him into the bulkhead. Medical equipment peppered him, bounced from the wall, went spinning crazily away. His trajectory away from the wall took him back into the console, winding him, but giving him something to hold onto.

The wave swept on into the bridge, shoving the dead man up against the bridge windows and causing Peters to bounce helplessly from the deck. She caught the back of one of the flight seats, holding on for dear life as momentum spun her around.

The wave swept on outward.

Starck, Smith, and Weir were startled as Justin's point-of-view monitor tried to clear for a moment, a vague image rolling amongst the static. Weir blinked, trying to clear his vision—he would have sworn that the image was of a man's face, screaming.

It couldn't have been, he told himself.

Justin's monitor cleared to static again. Starck opened her mouth to say something.

Miller's and Peters' monitors suddenly filled with static as well. The radio link hissed and went silent.

"What—" Smith started to say.

The *Lewis and Clark* began to rumble, a freight train sound that was incongruous out here in deep space.

The ship began to shudder and rattle. To Weir it felt as though reality was trying to twist.

The wave struck, ripping through the bridge. Metal was

screaming somewhere in the ship, the superstructure stressing as the gravity wave passed through.

Starck turned and ducked as a console flashed and sparked next to her. Behind Weir there was a loud bang as something shorted out, and he smelled ozone and burning insulation. The bridge lights flickered and dimmed.

Deeper in the ship, he could hear the sound of systems failing and metal tearing. Absurdly, he wondered if Peters' vid unit would be okay. It would tear her up to lose the recording of her son.

There was another sound too, shockingly familiar because he had spent so much time unconsciously on alert for it: the sound of air escaping into vacuum.

"The fuck was *that*?" Smith yelled.

His question did not receive an answer. A Klaxon was sounding now, emergency lights flashing. They were losing atmosphere. Starck had turned to her boards, getting answers from those that still worked. The bridge was filled with smoke that drifted lazily towards the hatch.

"We lost the starboard baffle," Starck said. She looked up, her face holding an urgency that bordered on panic. "The hull's been breached!"

The main pressure door to the bridge was closing, ready to seal them off. DJ would have to take his chances in the airlock bay, or wherever he was.

With a low grinding sound, the pressure door stopped, half-closed. Smoke drifted around it.

Smith was frantically checking a console, trying to get the door moving again. After a few moments he looked up, shaking his head. "The safety circuit's failed."

Weir stared at the drifting smoke, the stuck door. "We're losing atmosphere. . . ."

"There are pressure suits in the airlock," Starck snapped. *"Go!"*

They sprinted for the hatchway.

The smoke followed, a lazy snake.

Chapter Seventeen

Dark, dark, deep in the dark.

He was Within, suspended, the dark passing through him, stripping him naked, peeling out the contents of his mind, pouring the pieces of his soul into a pool that floated in Nothing.

I touch all things.

Who are you?

I am.

Another answer that made no sense.

The darkness had no end.

Innocence.

The concept seemed almost a curse. What was wrong with purity?

You know too well where the line is drawn.

Points of light pierced the darkness. There was a sound of pain, of anguish.

A circle of light, like fire breathed into the air. The darkness was not driven back.

You are not the one I need.

The points of light fell into the circle.

What am I, then?

Dangerous.

Lines of light fell from point to point.

Because of this?

Yes. We cannot suffer the innocent to live. It profits us nothing.

A five-pointed star within a circle. A shield, a hope.

Without knowing how he did it, he brought it close, trying to reintegrate himself in the warm soul-glow. *Lady be with me—*

Pfagh!

The darkness struck him, crushing, overpowering. All that remained of his consciousness fell away from him.

Silent and cold, Justin spun away through the darkness.

Cooper shot through the opening into the First Containment, slowing long enough to get his bearings as he approached the whirling tube. The sight sickened him, but it did not slow him down. Oriented, he kicked off again, sailing through the microgravity like an underpowered version of Superman, one arm flung out ahead.

He shot down the tube and into the Second Containment, growling, "Hold on, Baby Bear...."

Coolant was once again forming wandering globules. He splashed through several of them, splattering coolant left and right, making angry noises at the obstructions.

Reaching out, he managed to kill his velocity by grabbing the main console, an effort that almost dislocated his shoulder. He caught sight of Justin's safety line, taut across the room, and made his way to it, following it down into the main area of the Containment.

The line went all the way down to the Core.

It went into the Core.

"Oh my God," Cooper whispered.

The Core was a pulsing black mass poised in the middle of the gloom. It seemed almost alive, angry. Justin had somehow fallen into it, or been pulled in. The safety line had not slackened, which meant that it was still likely to be attached to him.

Cooper put his hand on the line.

It went slack. Cooper's heart skipped a beat and his skin felt so cold suddenly that he could have sworn his suit heater had quit.

The Core rippled and pulsed outwards, a cold black explosion. Cooper started to back off, his heart racing. There was another pulse, bigger this time.

Something light hurtled from the depths of the darkness. A human figure.

Justin.

Cooper kicked off, hurtling upward, his arms wide. Justin, limp as a dishrag, slammed into him, sending them both off on a new vector, the pulse from the Core providing additional impetus. Cooper turned his head frantically, tumbling them slightly. They were heading straight for one of the long control rods that lined the containment chamber, a fatal encounter if they struck it head on.

Cooper twisted, kicking out, trying to change their position. He finally managed to put them both into a slow backwards tumble, praying that it would be enough.

He clutched Justin tightly, closed his eyes and begged the gods for mercy.

He felt the control rod slide by beneath his backside, slick and cold. He almost cried with relief.

They slammed into the wall, rebounded, came up against the side of another control rod. Cooper was ready by then, holding on to Justin with one arm and gripping a long zero-g screwdriver in the other. He drove the business end of the screwdriver into the side of the control rod and hung on for dear life. It was a hell of a way to stop. Between hitting the wall and this ad hoc braking maneuver, Cooper figured he was going to be aching for the next two years.

Cooper extracted the screwdriver bit and put the tool away on his belt, turning his attention to Justin. He pulled the younger man close, looked him over.

"Justin, you talk to me, give me something here," Cooper said. Justin's head lolled to one side. The engineer was still breathing. There was no way to tell for sure until Justin's suit came off, but there were no overt signs of physical injury, no apparent bleeding. The suit was still secure, no visible holes or signs of air loss.

Cooper closed his eyes tightly, wondering if he could pray enough to bring them both out of this mess in one piece.

"Baby Bear," he said, softly, "don't do this . . . don't do this. . . ."

Clutching Justin to him, he kicked off again, aiming for the exit.

Behind him, the Core pulsed with dark malevolence.

Chapter Eighteen

Medical instruments and debris whirled lazily in the air, some bouncing gently from the walls, ceiling, deck. The last vibrations had subsided now.

Whatever had struck the *Event Horizon* had moved on, Miller realized. It did not seem likely to repeat itself any time soon. Cautiously, he rose out of his protective crouch, giving his suit a visual check as best he could.

He turned around, surveying the damage. The hatch was buckled and torn, the door hanging by one bent hinge. Some medical instruments had been buried in the walls, ceiling, and floor. Cabinets and lockers had been blown open, contents spilling out to add to the general airborne chaos.

No indication of air leaks. *Small mercies*, he thought.

Auto-keying his radio, he said, "Can anybody hear me?"

There was an almost immediate response from Smith. "Captain Miller."

Miller sighed and frowned, but it was more with relief than annoyance. "Smith, where the hell have you been?"

"We have a situation here," Smith said.

Miller suddenly felt ice cold.

*   *   *

As far as Weir was concerned at the moment, the best way to make a man feel clumsy and incompetent was to make him get into an EVA suit in a hurry. DJ was patiently helping him with the details, which meant that DJ was taking a terrible risk himself.

Starck was just completing her suit-up, getting her helmet in place and locked down. Smith had managed to be in a suit faster than Weir had ever imagined it could be done. His helmet was already on, and he was holding a conversation with Miller.

DJ slapped Weir's helmet onto his suit. Weir reached up to seal it, hearing the hiss. The radio was already active.

Smith was saying, "We lost the starboard baffle and the hull cracked. Our safety seals didn't close, the circuit's fried—"

"Do we have time for a weld?" Miller asked. To Weir the Captain sounded as steady as a rock. He envied Miller that cool detachment.

DJ was suiting up quickly now. Starck came over to Weir, checking his suit and making sure his helmet was properly sealed.

"We're losing pressure at two hundred and eighty liters a second," Smith said, "and our oxygen tanks ruptured. In three minutes our atmosphere will be gone. We are fucking dead."

"No one's dying on my watch, Smith!" Miller barked. His was a voice you would choose not to argue with. "What about the reserve tanks?"

"They're gone," Smith said.

There was a long silence. Weir pictured Miller racking his brain for a solution to the dilemma and failing to come up with anything acceptable. As far as Weir could tell, listening to the damage reports and Smith's pessimistic liturgy, there was only one option left to them.

"The *Event Horizon*," Weir said.

Starck, Smith, and DJ turned to stare at him.

"What?" Smith said.

Weir stepped towards Smith. "It still has air and reserve

power. We can activate gravity and life support.''

"No one's breathed that air in seven years," DJ said. "It could be contaminated."

"We can't stay in these suits," Starck said. "The air won't last."

"I'm not getting on that bastard," Smith said, sounding angrier and angrier. "We don't even know what happened on that ship."

Weir turned to the pilot, his face set. "It beats dying, Mr. Smith."

Miller closed his eyes again, tried not to sigh, opened his eyes. "Weir's right. Get on board the *Event Horizon*. I'll meet you at the airlock."

He started toward the ruined hatch as Smith said, "But—"

"You heard me, Smith." He stopped in the corridor, got his back up against the wall. "Peters, are you with me?"

I'm ahead of you," Peters said.

She moved across the main consoles, throwing switches, checking readouts. For all the design work thrown into the *Event Horizon*, the ship had some very standardized instrumentation. She had the boards figured out and operating.

"Bringing the thermal units online," she announced, pressing a keypad.

She turned to another part of the console, making sure she had her feet planted firmly on the deck. "Hold tight and prep for gees," she said, then counted to ten under her breath.

She pressed another keypad.

Beneath the decks, artificial gravity units ramped up, humming. Peters felt the rising fields as a pulsing, tingling sensation through her body. Suddenly she had weight again, not just mass.

The frozen corpse, aloft once again, arced down to the deck. Peters jumped back as it shattered on impact, scattering frozen flesh and blood across the deck.

In the Second Containment, Cooper heard the warning and aimed for the deck, coolant or no coolant, an effort to make certain Justin was safe. He almost made it all the way before the artificial gravity pulled the two of them down.

They hit the deck in a rain of coolant. Cooper held Justin close, trying to shield his faceplate with an arm.

The gray downpour ended abruptly, leaving them lying in a slick gray pool. Cooper propped Justin up, making sure he was still breathing, then scrabbled his way upright, using the console for leverage.

He looked down into the Second Containment, seeking the source of Justin's condition.

The Core rippled with blackness and seemed to turn in on itself, taking on a new solidity. Rings appeared around the main casing, spinning slowly. The dark energy seemed to bleed away to nowhere.

Cooper shook his head. None of this made any sense. None of it.

Something else caught his attention. Sections of Justin's safety line, across the Second Containment. They had spread a considerable length of rope around the place after Justin had emerged from the Core, but not all of it had come out.

He tracked the sections.

Both ended at the Core. Both were lying on the gantry, sheared through. There should have been a couple hundred meters more of the line, Cooper figured, between those shear points.

It was nowhere to be seen, but he knew exactly where it was, and the thought of what *might* have happened froze him, leeching his strength. He turned, his back against the console, and slid down until he was sitting in the coolant again.

Oh, Baby Bear, he thought, *where did you go?*

Chapter Nineteen

Miller raced through the *Event Horizon*, his feet pounding against the deck. Time was a critical factor now, and he had no time to waste in strolling down to the airlocks. This mission had gone to hell in a handbasket and it was going to take a miracle to pull them back from the edge.

He reached the airlocks just as Weir arrived, the rest of the *Lewis and Clark*'s crew coming behind him. Miller was mildly surprised. Weir's body language displayed an almost inhuman eagerness. Starck followed Weir into the ship, DJ arriving right behind her. Smith trailed in reluctantly, hanging back as much as he could. Miller glared at his pilot, but he no longer had any time to waste in cajoling the man along.

"Everybody okay?" Miller said, looking them over.

"We're all here," Starck said.

"Okay." Miller took a deep breath, knowing full well that none of his crew would like his next selected move. "Let's find out how much time we just bought."

"I still have to test the air," DJ said, hurriedly.

Miller shook his head. "No time. This is the only oxygen we've got for three billion klicks."

DJ stepped forward, lifting a hand. Miller did not expect the move to go much further than that. "And if it's contaminated?"

"I'll let you know," Miller said.

He undogged his helmet catches and heard the hiss of the seal opening. He exhaled slowly, then lifted the helmet off, taking a deep breath.

DJ was watching his face, unblinking.

Miller breathed out.

He smiled.

Chapter Twenty

The *Event Horizon* rippled with light and power, coming alive.

On the bridge, Weir moved easily between the different bridge stations, restoring power, bringing things back to life. Watching him, Miller found it hard to accept that the scientist had spent seven years away from his pet project. Even harder to accept that Weir had spent relatively little time aboard the vessel before its ill-fated maiden voyage. He seemed completely comfortable aboard the ship, oblivious to the signs of carnage around him.

Miller turned back to Starck, who had taken up residence at the communications workstation. She had spent the past ten minutes running one diagnostic routine after another, trying to ascertain the state of the communications equipment.

She looked up now. "The antenna array's completely fried. We've got no radio, no laser, no high-gain." She looked directly into his eyes, playing the brave soldier to the hilt. "No one's coming to help us." She coughed suddenly, covering her mouth. "This air tastes bad."

Miller had to agree with her on that score. "But you can breathe it."

"Not for long," she said.

"Not enough oxygen?"

"Oxygen is not the problem," Starck said.

"Carbon dioxide." Miller's voice was flat.

Starck nodded. "It's building up with every breath we take." She sat back, rubbing her face. "The CO_2 filters on the *Event Horizon* are shot."

Miller considered a couple of possibilities, then said, "We can take the filters from the *Clark*."

Starck nodded again. "I thought of that," she said, tapping her fingers on the communications station. "With the filters from the *Clark* we've got enough breathable air for twenty hours. After that we'd better be on our way home."

Miller nodded, accepting that judgment. "What about the life readings you picked up?"

Starck grimaced, then shrugged. "The *Event Horizon* sensors show the same thing—'bio-readings of indeterminate origin.' Right before the *Clark* got hit there was some kind of surge, right off the scale, but now it's back to its previous levels."

Miller knew he was trying to get blood from a stone with this line of questioning, but he had to find answers. If he was going to keep everyone alive, he needed all the information that could be gathered. He had not had all the information when the *Goliath* went out from under him, and it had cost lives.

"What's causing the readings?"

Starck looked back at the silent comms board, frowning. "Whatever it is, it's not the crew."

"So where are they?" He looked around, frustrated, feeling helpless. "We've been over every inch of this ship and all we've found is blood."

Weir had paused in his peregrinations around the bridge. At the moment, he was standing silently, looking at a bloody smear high up on one bulkhead. Miller looked up at it too. There were many more around the ship. The only complete corpse they had discovered so far was now packed piecemeal into a cryogenics unit in the hope that they could get it back to Earth for analysis and disposal. DJ had barely complained about cleaning up the mess.

Weir looked down from the bloody wall, then turned his head to look at Miller. There was something strange in Weir's eyes, but Miller pushed the thought aside. Right now everyone was a little weird, some worse than others.

"What happened here?" Miller asked.

Weir remained silent.

Chapter Twenty-one

Even with lights cutting into the darkness of it, the *Event Horizon* was a frightening beast of a ship, a huge construction that was difficult to comprehend. Against it, the *Lewis and Clark* was a speck, a pilot fish accompanying a whale.

Feeling like a brother to dust, Smith clung to the hull of the *Lewis and Clark*, bulky in full EVA gear and cautious as he moved forward, one magnetic boot at a time. This was a hell of a way to earn a pension, but at least it got him off the *Event Horizon*. There was something sick and unholy about that ship; he had been certain of that since Weir had started to explain what all this was about.

Just ahead of him, there was a long rip in the hull plating. The metal had buckled together, tearing like aluminum foil under the pressure of the wave that had struck the two ships. Vapor was still leaking slowly into space.

He knelt down carefully, taking a closer look, then keyed his suit radio. "Captain Miller, you copy?"

"I'm here, Smith," Miller said. *Jesus*, Smith thought, *am I sounding insecure or something?* Miller's tone was almost condescending. "How's the *Clark*?"

I'm fine, sir, doing okay out here. He bit his tongue. Miller was doing all he could. "I've found a two-meter fracture in the outer hull. We should be able to repair it and re-pressurize." He paused for a moment. "It's going to take some time."

"We don't have time, Smith. In twenty hours we run out of air."

That certainly put things into perspective.

"Understood," he said.

Out here all alone, then, which was fine, because he would rather be here than aboard that monstrosity of a spaceship. Neptune passed below him, a dizzying experience if he wanted to look in that direction. He kept his attention entirely on the *Lewis and Clark.*

He reached to his utility belt, extracting the basic patch applicator, emptying it into the tear. The compound went in almost as a gel, but quickly foamed and spread. Within moments it had hardened. The patch would be durable, though not pretty, and secure once it was riveted into place.

He tossed the empty applicator away, not watching to see it begin to fall in a decaying orbit toward Neptune. He reached down to the utility belt again, pulling out a zero-gravity nailgun. He began riveting the edges of the patch into place.

All tied to each other in one way or another, planet, man, and ships hurtled on through the darkness.

Chapter Twenty-two

Justin had retreated somewhere deep inside himself, Peters thought. He had seen something, heard something, been somewhere that his conscious mind could not accept, and this condition was his best defense. Cooper had not been able to fill in many of the details—he had been in a mild state of shock himself.

She looked down at Justin, and her heart ached for him. He was too young, too kind, for this to have happened to him. Perhaps he should never have been assigned to this particular vessel in the first place—at this age people ought to be confined to milk runs. Let the grizzled old combat veterans fly the desperate missions.

Justin was stretched out on a diagnostic table, covered with a thermal blanket. Looking at him, it was hard to believe that there was anything seriously wrong.

She looked up from Justin. DJ stood at the other side of the bed, watching her. She found his studiously neutral expression to be irritating.

"How is he?" she said, trying to push her mind away from the annoyance. DJ was doing everything he could. The mask he wore was nothing more than his way of coping with the situation.

"His vitals are stable," DJ said, slowly, "but he's unresponsive to stimuli. He might wake up in fifteen minutes. He might not wake up at all."

Peters looked down at Justin again. He seemed to be sleeping.

She turned away abruptly, squeezing her eyes shut, willing the pain back. There were things to be done. She headed for the bridge.

Chapter Twenty-three

Miller had gone so far as to issue an "at ease" command, but even that edict could not overcome the tension and exhaustion in his crew. There was too much evidence of mayhem, too much debris, too much blood. Too much of everything except time, air, and answers.

Weir was the exception amongst them. He had taken up a position at the briefing table, lounging there as though he hadn't a care in the world. Miller had expected the scientist to be falling apart by this point, given his earlier behavior. It could be that Weir was simply comfortable on board the *Event Horizon*, but that discounted the gory, battered state of the spacecraft.

Starck could barely sit still. Miller suspected that it was only the issue of their air supply that kept her from pacing about like a caged cat. Even so, she fidgeted constantly. More irritating was Cooper—he was bouncing that ball of his. Miller kept quiet about it; better he do that than come up with something wilder. DJ, meanwhile, sat quiet, sometimes glancing over at Peters, who was staring out of the bridge windows, hiding her emotions as best she could.

Miller turned to look at a video monitor. Smith was still working on the hull of the *Lewis and Clark*. Miller suspected that Smith could have been finished long ago—he just did not want to be back on board the *Event Horizon*.

Miller turned away from the monitor and faced his crew. He took a deep breath, wondering if he could get them out of this mess. He trusted them to pull together, and he figured Weir would pitch in, but the circumstances were wretched and their resources far too tight.

"Okay, people," he said, pitching his voice low enough to avoid being threatening while still maintaining authority, "there's been a change in the mission. In less than eighteen hours we will run out of breathable air. Our primary objective now is *survival*. That means we focus on repairing the *Lewis and Clark* and salvaging whatever will buy us more time."

He looked around at his crew. Weir was staring at him, an unnerving focus. Peters had turned around from the bridge windows to listen to him. This was not new information, but he was gratified that they could still follow the protocols.

"Our secondary objective," he went on, "is finding out what happened to this ship and its crew. Two months from now I fully intend to be standing in front of the good Admiral giving my report, and I'd like to have more than my dick in my hands." That brought a couple of weary smiles. No one was going to be cajoled by cheap humor, however. "DJ, take samples from these stains, compare them to medical records. I want to know whose blood this is. Peters, I want you to go through the ship's log, see if we can't find some answers."

Peters straightened up, nodding. "I can use the station in Medical, keep an eye on Justin."

"Fine," Miller said. He looked at Starck. "Starck. I want you to repeat the bio-scan."

Starck closed her eyes, sighing. "I'll just get the same thing—"

"Not acceptable," Miller snapped. He was not about to allow Starck to quit trying now. As soon as any of them quit trying, that person was as good as dead. "I want to know what's causing those readings. If the crew is dead, I want the bodies. I want them *found.*"

Starck sat for a few moments, thinking it through. Then she looked up at Miller, her expression determined. "I can reconfigure the scan for C-12, amylase proteins."

"Do it." Starck turned away, getting to work. Miller turned to the briefing table. "Dr. Weir."

Weir did not flinch away. "Yes."

"One of my men is down. I want to know what happened to him."

Cooper grabbed his ball out of the air with a loud smacking sound. "I told you," the rescue tech said anrgily. "He was inside the Core."

Weir was shaking his head, the relaxed look lost now. The scientist looked confused, juist as he had looked confused when Cooper had tried to explain what had happened earlier. At that point all they had on hand was chaos; Miller had hoped to get something more out of Weir during the briefing.

Cooper was silent for a few moments. Weir said nothing, intent on Cooper. Miller nodded at Cooper, giving his assent for Cooper to continue.

Cooper swallowed and tried to compose himself. "It was like . . . nothing was there." Cooper looked up at Miller, but found no cure for his helplessness there. "And then Justin appeared and then it . . . it was like . . ." Cooper was becoming unfocused, trying to find his way back into memory, putting words to the clutter of images. ". . . liquid. And then the rings started moving again and it froze solid."

"That's not physically possible," Weir snapped.

Cooper stared at him, shocked at Weir's tone. "Excuse me, Dr. Weir, *you* weren't there. So don't talk to me about physics."

Weir was set and determined. He leaned forward, onto the table. "Mr. Cooper, those rings only stop moving just before the gravity drive activates, If they weren't moving, that would mean the gateway was open—"

"Then that's what I saw," Cooper said, interrupting Weir. "The gateway was open."

"—and the gateway can't have been open," Weir continued, ignoring Cooper, "because the gravity drive was not activated."

Cooper turned to Miller, a desperate look on his face. "Skipper, you're not going to listen to this fucking pogue—"

"It can't just turn on by itself," Weir snapped.

Cooper turned angrily, rising from his seat. His right arm snapped back, forward, sending the ball at Weir's face. To Miller's surprise, the scientist ducked fast, the ball doing no more than ruffling his hair. The ball struck the rear bulkhead and caromed off into the deck and back into the air.

"Cooper!" Miller reached out and plucked the ball from the air. Cooper sat down heavily, boneless. Miller gave Weir a hard look. "Dr. Weir, Justin may die. Whatever happened to him could happen to all of us."

Weir hesitated for far too long, a pause that told Miller that the scientist was trying to sugarcoat the truth. Finally Weir shrugged and said, "Maybe Mr. Cooper saw an optical effect caused by . . ." Weir frowned, hesitating again. "Gravitational distortion."

Cooper glared at Weir. His hands were clenched into fists. "I know what I saw and it wasn't a fucking 'optical effect'!"

"*Mr. Cooper!*" Miller barked. Cooper subsided, glaring at Weir. This was all he needed—Cooper acting like Smith. He was faintly glad that Smith was elsewhere, working on the *Lewis and Clark*. Miller turned his attention to Weir, who was warily resuming his seat. " 'Gravitational distortion?' "

Weir hesitated for a moment, watching Cooper. His scrutiny made no difference in Cooper's attitude or posture. Reluctantly, he looked at Miller. "If a burst of gravity waves escaped from the Core, they could distort space-time. They could have made Justin seem to disappear. They could also have damaged the *Lewis and Clark*."

As far as Miller was concerned, there was something missing, something Weir was avoiding saying. "What could cause them?" Weir was silent, staring helplessly at Miller. "What's in the Core?"

"It's complicated . . ." Weir trailed off, looking abashed at the weakness of this answer.

"How much time do you need?" Miller said, taking several steps closer to Weir, leaning down on the briefing table, using his clenched fists for support. "We have seventeen hours and forty-two minutes. Now . . . what is in the Core?"

Weir was silent for too long again. Miller began to consider less civil methods of getting information out of Weir. Suddenly, the scientist seemed to make a decision.

Weir sat forward, staring wildly at Miller.

"A black hole," Weir said.

Chapter Twenty-four

Miller and Starck stood at the end of the walkway into the Second Containment, watching the Core uneasily. Neither of them trusted Weir's pet Tinkertoy. The rings were moving slowly, quietly, but the Core itself had an eerie rippling effect, a sense of a great dark power somehow confined to a small space.

All around them, power hummed and sang of enormous energies. Miller felt dwarfed in this space.

Weir, by contrast, was at ease again, walking around the Core, inspecting it, looking it over like a loving father. Miller almost expected him to reach out and pet the thing.

Weir turned and looked up at them. "When a star dies, it collapses in on itself, becomes so dense that nothing can escape its gravity, not even light. It becomes a black hole."

Starck was staring at the Core, unwavering. "The most destructive force in the universe," she whispered. "And you created one."

"Yes," Weir said. He seemed infernally cheerful. "We can use that power to fold space-time."

Not as much power as Weir would like everyone to think,

Miller reflected. He was ready to bet that Weir's Core actually dealt with quantum black holes as postulated in the work of Stephen Hawking and others in the last two decades of the twentieth century. Given Weir's ability to produce one on cue and trap it within the Core, there was enough power there to fold space-time nicely. It had been speculated that the 1907 Tunguska incident had been caused by a quantum black hole rather than a meteorite.

Either way, Weir had a tiger by the tail in here, and he knew it. *You arrogant son of a bitch*, Miller thought.

"It would take the *Lewis and Clark* a thousand years to reach our closest star. The *Event Horizon* could be there in a day."

Sotto voce to Miller, Starck said, "If it worked."

Weir smiled. "You can come down. It's perfectly safe."

Miller and Starck exchanged looks, then walked down to the Core. Everything in here, with the exception of the Core itself, seemed to be coated with coolant. It gave Miller the uncomfortable feeling of walking willingly into the belly of the whale. *Hello, my name is Jonah, I am an appetizer.*

Somewhere the idea had lost its humorous edge.

Miller and Starck stopped before the Core, staring up at it, getting a closer look at the machinery as it moved around. Even at this close a range, the Core played optical tricks. Miller felt vaguely sick.

"You let us board this ship," Miller said to Weir, "and you didn't tell **us**?"

Weir turned to face Miller, folding his arms. "My instructions were to brief you on a need-to-know basis. Given our current situation, you need to know."

Miller stared at Weir, barely able to comprehend the man's attitude. "I want this room sealed. The Second Containment is off limits."

Weir was trying to stare Miller down, but it was not working. "There's no danger. The black hole is contained behind three magnetic fields. It's under control."

"Under control?" Miller growled. He waved an arm, pointing to somewhere out beyond the confines of the *Event Horizon*. "My ship is in pieces. Justin is dying." Miller took a deep breath, trying to rein his temper in without success. "No one goes near that thing."

Miller turned around and started back up the walkway. Starck stared at Weir for a moment more, then she followed her captain.

Weir watched them leave.

Overhead, the power sang.

Chapter Twenty-five

Peters squeezed her eyes shut and rubbed at her face, trying to blot out, for a moment at least, the tedious log visuals from the bridge flight recorder. Captain Kilpack and his crew had been meticulous about making log entries, but had not had much of any consequence to record.

She sat back, knowing she was starting to fade, and growing angry at doing so, even though she knew that was unreasonable. It would not have bothered her so much if she had something to show Miller. There was nothing yet.

Another structural status report. She sighed.

The lights flickered. Startled, she looked up, but the lights had steadied again. She looked back down at her screen.

Behind her, something made a rustling sound, like something moving over paper. She turned around, slowly. "Justin?"

Justin was still lying on the examination table, a sheet covering him. He had not moved or woken.

Something had made the sound.

The hairs rose on the back of her neck and she felt her arms breaking out in goosebumps. Cautiously, she reached out and grasped a scalpel from the instrument tray that DJ had set out for any further emergencies.

The sound started again, became clearer, became the sound of someone scrabbling at plastic, trying to break through with nothing more than fingernails and determination.

She stood up, walked past Justin, following the sound. The examination tables were covered in plastic sheeting, never having been readied for use.

The plastic around the last table was moving, something writhing beneath it. Not certain why she was doing so, she reached out and grasped the edge of the plastic cover, pulling it back, needing to know what was under there, what was calling her. . . .

Denny.

She gasped, suddenly weak, nerveless. The scalpel slipped from her fingers, struck the deck, bounced with a tinny noise.

Denny. He looked up at her from the table, his waist and legs still beneath the plastic, looked up at her and giggled in that way that he had, amused at a world that insisted on being silly to his perspective.

He reached up to her, and she remembered the vid she had been watching on the *Lewis and Clark*. She should pick him up, she thought, that's what Mom does, playing horsey.

''Mommy . . .'' Denny said, and he giggled again, as though this was just the best game in the world. His eyes shone, and she spilled over with love for him.

She started to pull the plastic further back, knowing she had to get him out from under there and that they could figure out the explanations later.

Then she saw what she had missed before. Where Denny's atrophied legs should have been, beneath the plastic, something was squirming frantically, like a bag of angry snakes, the plastic pulsing up and down.

Horrified, she dropped the plastic sheet, backing away. This could not have been Denny. Her son was on Earth, with his father.

''Peters?''

She turned too fast, almost losing her balance. DJ was standing in the hatchway, holding a collection of blood sample containers in rubber-gloved hands. His usual mask had slipped a little, revealing concern.

She turned back toward Denny.

The table was empty. Her son, or whatever was masquerading as her son, was gone. She looked back at DJ again.

"What's wrong?" he asked, putting the blood samples aside.

"I . . ." Peters started. She hesitated, trying to clear her mind. The images were trying to fade, becoming elusive. She squeezed her eyes shut, shuddering. "I'm very tired, that's all. It's nothing."

She made her way back to the workstation, trying to focus on her work.

It's nothing.

Chapter Twenty-six

Right now EVA was not precisely the thing Cooper wanted to do, despite his earlier eagerness. If anything, he would have preferred being in a Gravity Couch, totally out of it and well on the way back to Earth aboard the *Lewis and Clark*. This mission was totally, crazily, out of hand.

The one positive thing here was the size of the *Event Horizon*. That meant more airlock bays, which got around having the umbilicus in the way.

The inner airlock door hissed open and Smith stepped into the bay, undogging his helmet and pulling it off. His hair was matted down, slick with sweat.

"You been out there a long time," Cooper said, looking him over. "Trying to break my record?"

Smith sat down heavily on a bench, getting his gloves off. "I'd rather spend the next twelve hours outside than another five minutes in this can."

Cooper made a moue of disgust. "You don't need to tell me that. I pulled a lot of ops in my time, seen decompression, radiation . . . but what I saw today . . ."

Cooper trailed off, unable to say any more. He could not

push the images out of his mind, no matter how he tried.

"How is Justin?" Smith asked, interrupting the silence.

Cooper shook his head. "Same."

Smith opened his suit, then reached down to get his boots off. An EVA suit keeps you alive but makes you smell very, very bad in the process.

Suddenly, Smith said, "When I was a kid, my mother used to tell me I was gonna go to a bad place. And she was right." Smith's eyes were filled with a fervor that Cooper found more than a little spooky. "This ship, it's crazy, you know. I mean, trying to go faster than light, that's like the Tower of Babel. You know what God did to the Tower of Babel, don't you? He cast it down."

Cooper sighed, shaking his head. "Smith, we got *enough* shit going on without you going biblical on me."

Cooper picked up his helmet, put it on, and sealed it, hearing the hiss. Without waiting for Smith to check him over, he walked over to the airlock, hit the door control, and ducked through.

All of a sudden, being outside had become very, very attractive.

Chapter Twenty-seven

Miller, DJ, and Weir had gathered behind Peters as she recalled the last entry in the *Event Horizon* log. She had found nothing useful so far.

"This is the final entry in the ship's log," she said, and pressed the play control.

The video display cleared. Captain Kilpack appeared on the screen, sitting in the center seat. He looked excited, as well he should; this was the main event in the *Event Horizon*'s maiden voyage. His crew, all eighteen of them, were gathered behind him. A few solemn faces, many smiles.

Kilpack said, "I want to say how proud I am of my crew. I'd like to name my station heads Chris Chambers, Janice Rubin, Dick Smith, Tom Fender, and Stacie Collins. We have reached safe distance and are preparing to engage the gravity drive and open the gateway to Proxima Centauri."

"I wonder if they made it?" Miller said, quietly.

On the screen, Kilpack raised a hand in salute and said, "*Ave atque vale*. Hail and farewell."

Little did they know, Miller thought.

There was a burst of static across the screen. At first Miller thought the log disc had simply run its course, but then realized that it would then have simply stopped playing, shutting off the system. There was something else on the disc.

A terrible sound came pouring from the speakers, shrieking and inhuman, something out the depths of their nightmares. Peters yelped and reached for the gain slider, cutting the racket down.

To Miller, there was more than static on the screen. There was something moving inside the image. He reached out, tapping the pause control. He squinted at the screen, trying to resolve the image in the frozen frame. There was definitely something there, but he could not make it out at all now.

Peters was squinting at the frame too.

"What is that?" he asked her.

Peters shook her head. "I can run the image through a series of filters, try to clean it up."

There was a chance that they might learn something useful from the scrambled section of the disc. Miller nodded. "Proceed."

Without warning, the lights faded out slowly. Emergency lighting came on, illuminating them with a dim, reddish wash.

"A power drain," DJ said. Miller had to agree—something had been activated. He had a terrible suspicion about the reason for the drain.

"The Core!" Weir snapped, turning to Miller.

"Go!" Miller said.

Weir ran for the door.

"The rest of you stay here," Miller said, before DJ could head for the door. "I don't want anyone else going near that thing."

Miller took off after Weir.

He caught up with the scientist halfway down the main corridor, surprised at how fast Weir was able to move. They ran together through the First Containment and down the tunnel into the Second Containment, not waiting for the main door to open fully, squeezing by as soon as they could, not an easy trick for a man as tall and broad-shouldered as Miller.

"What's causing the drain?" Miller asked, as Weir went over to the main console.

"The magnetic fields are holding," Weir said, examining the readouts. He shook his head, looking baffled. "Maybe a short in the fail-safe circuit. I'll check it out."

Weir turned away from the console and opened a wall panel. To Miller's surprise, there were tools and flashlights inside. Weir handed tools to Miller, and waved him over to an access panel on the wall. They set to work silently, removing bolts and magnetic clamps.

Behind the access panel was a cramped-looking duct. Miller could see circuitry and modules inside as he bent down to look. The duct seemed to go for quite a distance.

He looked at Weir, dubious. "I hope you know what you're doing."

"Of course," Weir said. To Miller, he sounded as though he believed it too. Miller handed him a flashlight and a small, wrapped toolkit.

Weir tossed the flashlight and tools into the duct, then hauled himself inside. He almost filled the duct, but he seemed to have no trouble moving.

Miller shook his head. Weir was a walking contradiction.

Weir's boots vanished from sight.

Chapter Twenty-eight

The air in the operations duct was even more stale than the air circulating in the main part of the *Event Horizon*. Weir managed to tolerate it with difficulty—there was a job to do, and the sooner he did it, the sooner he would be out of there. He wished he had had a chance to sample real Earth air once more before coming out here, but he had not been off Daylight Station for years.

He had found himself unable to conceive of taking a journey back down the length of Skyhook One.

His breathing echoed in the cramped duct.

He crept forward, counting off circuit panels for Miller's benefit. "E–Three . . . E–Five . . . E–Seven . . . where are you . . . ?"

Starck had settled into a routine at the engineering board, trying to hammer the bio-scan into behaving itself. So far nothing had seemed to help.

A yellow light began flashing in the upper left corner of the console. Starck stared, a feeling of dread stealing over her. New lights joined the first—more yellows, greens.

"What is—" she started.

The bio-scan flickered to life, the meters immediately pegging at the end of the scale on all readouts.

She hit the intercom switch. "Captain, the bio-scan just went off the scale."

She shook her head.

Something bad was going on here.

DJ made it across the medical bay in record time, only to realize that there was little he could do at the moment. Justin was in the throes of an epileptic seizure, thrashing about on the examination table.

DJ leaned over him, ready to intervene if Justin's seizure showed signs of being dangerous or of throwing him to the deck. This might be a breakthrough point too, a sign that Justin was coming out of the coma.

"Justin!" DJ said, on the off chance that his patient was regaining consciousness. "Can you hear me? Justin!"

There was something going on. Justin's mouth was working as he tried to speak, and his eyes were open, albeit unfocused. DJ leaned in towards him, trying to hear.

Justin suddenly arched, all of his muscles becoming rigid, as though he were being electrocuted. DJ looked up, alarmed.

"He's coming," Justin hissed. His voice sounded broken, a remnant of the torturer's art.

DJ felt cold. "Who? Who's coming?"

"The dark!" Justin hissed. Something bubbled in his voice.

It might have been laughter.

There you are," Weir said.

Module E-12 was making a curious spitting and fizzing sound, very faint, but enough to indicate a potentially serious problem.

Weir produced a screwdriver from the toolkit, opening up the module in a few moments. The cause of the problem was immediately evident—one of the circuit boards was quietly frying itself, a handful of sparks flying off. Weir reached into the module and yanked the board out.

He pulled more tools out of the kit, and set to work. These modules were triple-redundant throughout the *Event Horizon*, but the removal of a board meant installing a bypass so that the system would not go looking for the missing chunk of circuitry. Getting the bypass in place was a minute or two of cramped, uncomfortable work.

As he started to back up, readying himself to get out of the duct, his flashlight began to flicker. He grunted, annoyed at the timing, and banged it against the duct wall, making the metal boom. Miller had handed him one of the *Event Horizon*'s flashlights, which might explain why this one was dying now. The flashlights had been equipped with lithium-ion batteries, but even those had limits when it came to their life.

The light dimmed again. He shook it, but it did not help. The flashlight gave a last fitful glow and went out, plunging him into darkness.

"Um, Captain Miller?" Weir said, slowly. "I seem to have a problem with my light."

There was no answer from his radio, or along the duct.

Somewhere in the pitch darkness, far away and far too close, there was the sound of a single drip of water. Weir felt cold, alone, ready to panic.

"Captain Miller?" he whispered.

He felt as though he was falling. He knew that could not be so. The artificial gravity had been turned on.

Water dripped again, echoing in the darkness. Weir closed his eyes, his breathing difficult.

"*Billy.*"

A woman's voice, as though at the bottom of a cavern. Weir looked up, opening his eyes, seeing only darkness. He knew that voice, knew it all too well even now.

"Billy," Claire said, her voice soft by his ear. "Come to me."

She could not be here. His breath came in a ragged gasp. Claire could not be here.

The walls pressed in upon him.

"Claire?" he whispered. His voice echoed away into the darkness. He banged the flashlight against the side of the duct, over and over, trying to make it work, giving in to desperation.

"Be with me," Claire whispered, and he almost screamed.

The flashlight flickered to life.

Wet hair hanging like seaweed in her ashen face, Claire stared at him, inches away.

"Forever," she said softly.

Chapter Twenty-nine

Miller bent down to look into the duct, wondering what was going on with Weir. The darkness inside the duct seemed to be total, which meant Weir had gone pretty far into the thing. The radio link had been silent for minutes, but he could not be sure if that was because Weir had not said anything since crawling into the duct, or if there was something in the duct that was blocking radio signals.

He was about to straighten up when all of the lights went out. Even the main console had gone black.

He took a deep breath, focusing on calm, keeping the storm of panic away from himself. He bent down again, finding the edge of the duct with his fingers.

"We just lost all power in here," he called into the duct. He heard his voice echo somewhere deep inside, but there was no answer. "Dr. Weir?"

Nothing.

He straightened up, trying to see something in the darkness. To his surprise, he was successful.

The surprise gave way to fear. He knew he was looking toward the Core, but the red glow that he was seeing was not something he would have expected from the Core in its normal state.

He took several steps back.

The glow at the Core resolved into a humanoid figure consumed by fire. The sounds of inferno filled the air, and Miller felt a wave of heat pass over him.

The figure lifted a blazing arm, fire dripping from it like water, pointing at Miller.

The holocaust whispered, *"Don't leave me. . . ."*

Miller squeezed his eyes shut, his chest hollow.

When he opened his eyes again, the burning man was gone.

Chapter Thirty

Cooper was still outside, but everyone else had gathered back on the bridge. Miller figured he probably looked about as burned out as the rest of the crew by now. Even Weir, sitting back at the briefing table, looked thrashed, his easy manner gone away completely. Weir had emerged from the duct looking like death warmed over.

DJ was mooching about on the bridge, a scalpel in his hand that he was unconsciously flicking against the leg of his flight suit. Miller could not figure out how DJ had so far failed to draw blood.

"Carbon dioxide poisoning produces hallucinations, impaired judgment—" DJ was saying.

They had been around this particular track once already, trying to put Miller's vision into some sort of psychological pigeonhole. "Goddammit, DJ, it was *not* a hallucination!" Miller turned to Weir, who was staring blankly at the two of them. "Dr. Weir, you were in the duct, you heard it."

"No," Weir said. His voice sounded rusty.

"You must have seen something."

"No," Weir said. His expression never changed. Miller

knew he was lying, but he was not sure that Weir was lying about what Miller had experienced. "I saw nothing."

"I did," Peters said.

They all turned to look at her. She looked from one to the next, looking uncertain.

"About an hour ago," she said. She looked at DJ, apologetic. "In Medical. I saw my son. He was lying on one of the examination tables and his legs were . . ."

She trailed off, working to contain her emotions.

"Isn't it possible," Weir said coldly, "that you were traumatized by finding the body on the bridge?"

Peters' head snapped up and she gave him an angry glare. "I've seen bodies before. This is different."

"Peters is right," Miller said, folding his arms and looking down at Weir. He wondered what the scientist had seen in the duct, if he had seen anything at all. "It's not like something in your head, it's real. Smith, what about you?"

Smith was leaning against the hatchway, his arms folded and a troubled expression on his face. To Miller, he looked about ready to bolt from the *Event Horizon* at a moment's notice.

"I didn't see anything," Smith said, truculent, "and I don't have to see anything. But I'll tell you something—this ship is *fucked*."

Weir turned to look at Smith, a dismissive expression in place. "Thank you for that scientific analysis, Mr. Smith."

Miller could have kicked Weir for his blatant attempt to provoke Smith. All they needed now was a physical battle, not that Weir stood a chance of bringing Smith down.

"You don't need to be a fucking scientist to figure it out!" Smith yelled, taking a step toward Weir, who regarded the pilot with a stony expression.

"Smith!" Miller growled. Out of the corner of his eye, he saw DJ moving closer to Smith.

Smith ignored his captain. "You break all the laws of physics," he snarled at Weir, "you think there won't be a price? You already killed the last crew—"

DJ reached out and put a hand on Smith's shoulder.

Ah shit! Miller thought. Of all the moves DJ could have made.

Smith swung around in a flash, slamming DJ back. DJ twisted away, grasping Smith's flight suit with one hand, using the pilot's momentum against him. Continuing his movement, DJ slammed Smith up against the bulkhead, not attempting to soften the impact.

His hand blurring, DJ raised the scalpel, pressing the tip of it just below Smith's ear. Smith froze in place.

"DJ!" Miller yelled, crossing the bridge. He would never have expected this sort of thing from DJ, certainly nothing as fast as this.

DJ took a deep breath, shuddering. He let the scalpel fall to the deck as he stepped back, releasing Smith. DJ looked helplessly at Miller, at Smith. "I'm sorry, I . . . I don't know why I did that."

"Carbon dioxide," Weir said, his tone sarcastic.

Smith lunged at Weir, fists swinging. The scientist flinched back. "He's fucking lying! You know something—"

Miller got in front of Smith, grabbed him by the upper arms, squeezed. "That's it, that's enough for one day, Smith!" He glared into the pilot's eyes, giving him a look that threatened to shred the younger man on the spot. "I need you back on the *Clark*, I need you calm, I need you using your head. You make a mistake out there, nobody's getting home, you understand?"

Smith had started to try shaking Miller off, but the litany and the expression stopped that. Smith seemed to want to look everywhere but at his captain, but, in the finish, he met Miller's eyes. Miller was glad to see Smith cooling off, even relaxing a little.

Finally Smith said, in a calmer voice, "Sir."

"We're a long way from home and we're in a bad place," Miller said, letting the pilot go. "Let's not make it worse."

Miller shook his head. He needed a few minutes to walk off the anger and the growing stress. Without saying anything more, he left the bridge, finding his way into one of the corridors that lined this end of the ship.

He was aware of Starck following him. Unfinished business, probably, most likely something he ought to take care of. He wanted nothing more than a couple of minutes alone, but he was not going to get that.

"Miller," Starck said.

Miller did not break his pace, merely kept going, determinedly hewing to his course to nowhere. "What is it, Lieutenant?"

"I've been studying the bio-scan," she said, hurrying to match pace with him, "and I've got a theory."

Miller raised an eyebrow. "Proceed."

"I think there's a connection between the readings and the hallucinations, like they were all part of a defensive reaction, sort of an immune system—"

Miller increased his pace, still avoiding looking at her. "I don't need to hear this."

Starck pushed her pace, trying to keep up with Miller. The effort left her almost running to match Miller's long strides.

"You've got to listen!" she said.

Miller's course had taken them through the ship into an airlock bay. Miller stopped abruptly, causing her to stumble. He turned to face her. "To what? What are you saying? This ship is *alive*?"

Starck shook her head. "I didn't say that. I said the ship is reacting to us. And the reactions are getting stronger. It's getting worse."

Miller was breathing hard, trying to examine the concept rationally, unable to fathom it. "Starck, do you know how crazy that sounds? It's impossible."

Her stare was unwavering. "That doesn't mean it's not true."

Miller looked at her for a long time, silent. Finally, he said, "Don't tell anyone what you just told me."

Chapter Thirty-one

Time passing.

The lights flickered throughout the ship.

Smith had left the *Event Horizon*.

A dark sensation swept through the ship. If Miller had been willing to accept the notion, he might have thought the ship was breathing, displaying signs of life.

They were all becoming afraid of the *Event Horizon*, Weir thought, sitting at the gravity drive workstation. Miller was barely talking, and Starck was constantly glancing around herself, always checking the corners as she moved. Peters had returned to Medical, but she had been frightened, either for Justin or of what she might see.

DJ and Starck were still on the bridge. DJ was scraping blood samples from the bulkheads, being as thorough as possible in the time they had left. Starck was trying to make herself useful, but between the lack of communication and the difficulties with the bio-scan, she was frustrated and angry. She had chased off after Miller, obviously with something on her mind. She had returned to the bridge looking even more frustrated than before.

For his part, Weir had settled down with the gravity drive workstation and a nice embedding diagram. It rotated slowly on the display in front of him, while he gazed at it, unraveling the intricacies of it in his mind. The funnel-shaped wireframe image could tell him a great deal, under normal circumstances. For the moment, it was not telling him anything he did not already know. It was hard to concentrate right now. He could not get the image of Claire out of his mind. Old wounds had opened up again, old nightmares.

Starck walked up behind him, leaned down over his shoulder, looking at the display. "What is that?"

"A phase-space model of the gateway," he said, not caring if she understood him or not.

She looked at the embedding diagram for a moment, watching it spin. "Tell me something. If the ship's engine is a black hole, when you power it up, it sort of . . . to put it in the simplest terms, it sucks the ship in and then spits the ship out somewhere else."

"Well," Weir said, trying to adjust to her simplistic perspective, "basically, yes."

"Except the *Event Horizon* got spit out seven years too late."

Weir nodded. "It's possible." He waved at the wireframe model. "If I reconstruct what happened when the gravity drive was activated—"

"It could tell us where the ship's been for those seven years."

"Exactly," Weir said. *Thank you for rambling through the obvious*, Weir thought. He was growing impatient with Starck and her questions.

She was studying the wireframe intently, following the curves and lines with her eyes. The sides of the funnel never quite touched, never quite went anywhere, which was just as it should be.

"That's the black hole," Starck said.

"Yes," Weir said, softly. "The singularity." He half-smiled, suddenly enjoying himself, focusing on one of his favorite subjects. "The curvature of space becomes infinite and physics . . . physics just stops. A region of pure and un-mitigated chaos.''

Starck was looking at him, almost curious, almost amused. "Why, Dr. Weir, I think you're in love."

"Hmm," Weir said, absently, lost in his rapture. "Claire used to tell me I loved the *Event Horizon* more than I loved her. I told her that wasn't true, I just knew the *Event Horizon* better, that's all."

"Claire is your wife?" Starck sounded as though she was warming to him, he noted. Nothing like the suggestion of domesticity to break the ice.

Flatly, he said, "She was. She died."

Starck almost recoiled, shocked. "I'm sorry."

Weir did not bother to respond. He kept his eyes on the shifting wireframe.

Behind them, DJ said, "Do you think you can give me a hand with this?"

Without replying, Starck moved away from Weir's station, joining DJ. Whatever ice had been broken had just as quickly been refrozen, which was just as well by Weir.

He continued to watch the wireframe.

Suddenly, galvanized, he sat forward. The wireframe was distorting, changing in a way that he had never seen before. The funnel was opening out beyond the singularity and staying stable, forming some kind of wormhole.

"Impossible," he whispered, shaking his head. "The gate-way never closed . . . it's still *open*. . . ."

He sat back, chilled.

If the gate was open, what was coming through it?

Chapter Thirty-two

Somewhere in her dreamworld, shadows were beating sticks on oil tanks, causing a great booming to resound through the desert landscape of her sleep. The sound was growing closer and closer, deafening her.

Peters woke with a start, wiping at her mouth where she had drooled a little. She had fallen asleep in one of the medical section's chairs and now had back and neck aches to go with the exhaustion.

Everything was fuzzy, unfocused. Her ears were ringing. She looked around, trying to remember. . . .

"Justin?" she said, pushing herself out of the chair.

There, in the shadows. Justin had somehow fallen from the examination table, taking the sheet with him. Suddenly hopeful, she crossed over to the untidy jumble of person and linen, and pulled back the edge of the sheet.

Justin was not beneath the sheet. The sheet had been draped over a pair of nitrogen tanks.

She looked around, wildly. "Justin!"

No answer.

Off to one side, a bio-scan display was just starting up.

There was a familiar metallic pounding in the distance, somewhere in the darkness of the *Event Horizon*. It echoed through the ship, growing louder. She had heard that sound in her dreams, the crashing sound of the shadows as they came.

Terror swelled up in her. Whatever it was, it was coming toward Medical, coming towards *her*. She sprinted for the hatch, wheeled right, and ran like the wind, her mind empty of everything except the need to get away.

The booming, thundering sound crashed on after her. She thought she felt the shadows closing around her, reaching for her. Her heart was pounding, her breath coming in short gasps.

She sprinted onto the bridge, turned around, slammed the pressure door, bolting it. The sound was momentarily cut off.

She turned around. DJ and Starck were at one side of the bridge, working on the bloodstains. Weir was at the other side of the bridge, but she couldn't tell on first glance what he was doing. They had all turned toward her, staring.

DJ started toward her. "What's wrong?"

Peters was gasping, winded from her run. "You didn't hear it? You must have heard it!"

"Heard what?" Starck said.

She could not believe it. She was shaking, terrified, but it was beginning to seem that the evidence of her own senses was in doubt. She took a deep breath, willing herself to relax, starting to loosen up.

Crash.

The door shook with the impact. Peters shrieked, whirling around, backing up into DJ.

The door boomed again, over and over, growing louder and louder. There were rattles interspersed now, parts of the door mechanism and structure loosening, rivets popping. The metal was groaning.

Starck had her hands over her ears, grimacing. Peters screamed again, rage and terror and pain mixing together. The crashes were coming closer and closer together now, impossibly loud.

"What is it?" DJ yelled at her.

She had no idea. How was she supposed to know? "Make it stop!" she screamed at him.

DJ stood by her, shaking his head, lost for answers.

Weir had walked away from his console, she noticed. His face was a blank mask, a sleepwalker's face. He walked slowly toward the door, seemingly oblivious to the thundering and vibration.

Starck went after him. "What are you doing?" Weir had reached the door, his hand held out. "No!"

She dove toward him, grabbing his arm. Blankly, he tried to shake off her grip, but she had managed to get him into a wristlock, twisting his arm back. He swung himself around toward Starck, raising his other hand, his face furious now.

The pounding ceased abruptly. The quiet was brutal, frightening, a weight that descended upon the room. Peters' ears were ringing, feeling as though they had been stuffed with cotton wool.

Weir and Starck remained frozen in their violent dance.

Something lifted from Weir. His face cleared. He lowered his hand, staring at Starck.

"In our current environment, Dr. Weir," she said, "self-control is an asset."

Peters tried to slow her breathing, stop the shaking. She could not afford to be weak now. Put off the reaction as long as possible, she thought, she could spend some time healing in the tank and get the rest over with when they got back to Earth.

Weir stared at Starck. "I'm all right," he said. "Please."

Keeping her eyes on him, Starck released the scientist and stepped back.

Somewhere in the distance, the pounding started again. This time it was moving away from them, deeper into the ship. Even at a distance, the sound terrified Peters. Something unknown was out there. A monster without explanation.

There was a loud beep from one of the consoles—the ship systems workstation, she remembered as she turned. A light was flashing. DJ left Peters and went over to the workstation, looking it over.

"What is it?" Starck said.

DJ looked around, baffled. "The forward airlock."

Starck keyed the radio. "Miller, Smith, Cooper, any of you in the airlock?"

Miller's voice came back, distracted. "That's a negative, Starck."

Peters' mind cleared for a moment, and she remembered, swearing at herself for forgetting in the first place.

"Justin," she said.

There was a general scramble for the pressure door then, and to hell with whatever was out there. They left Weir standing in the middle of the bridge, forgotten.

Peters raced through the corridors, DJ and Starck trying to keep pace with her. She was growing frantic again, wondering just what was going on with Justin. If he had been affected the way that Weir had, there was no telling what he could be doing now.

They raced into the forward airlock bay.

Justin was there, moving slowly, sleepwalking. He stepped into an open airlock, turning. He was not wearing a suit.

Peters tried to increase her speed, running across the bay, screaming, "Justin, no!" at the top of her lungs, feeling the lining of her throat inflaming with the force of her shout.

Justin stared at her, his eyes cold and dead. He reached out to the controls on the inside of the airlock.

The hatch hissed shut. Peters slammed into it, screaming at Justin, pounding her fists on the metal.

She slid to the floor.

Chapter Thirty-three

It was getting to be crowded out here, Miller thought. He, Cooper, and Smith had ended up together on one section of the *Lewis and Clark*'s hull, surrounded by an assortment of zero-g tools.

Cooper and Smith unbolted an access panel. Together they lifted it, moving it aside, letting it float nearby while they attended to the job at hand. The compartment beneath the panel was a mess of scorched wiring and battered components.

"We'll have to re-route through the port conduit to the APU," Cooper said, shining a light down into the compartment.

Smith grunted. "What about the accumulator?"

The radio pinged, and then Starck was saying, "Come in, Miller."

Miller looked up from the work at hand, annoyed at the interruption. "What's going on in there, Starck?"

"Justin's in the airlock," Stark said.

Miller froze. DJ had not been very hopeful about Justin, and Peters had basically entered a state of denial, hoping for the best, expecting the worst.

"What?" Miller said.

Cooper and Smith were watching him intently, their work forgotten.

Starck said, "He's awake, he's in the airlock, he's not wearing a suit."

Jesus Christ, Miller thought, *it just gets crazier*. He wanted the insanity to stop just long enough for them to get home.

Grabbing a handhold, he swung himself to face Cooper. "Stay here! Don't stop working!"

"Captain," Cooper snapped back, "you need me on this!"

The last thing Miller needed right now was for Cooper to start grandstanding over Justin. "Fix this ship, Cooper, or we'll all die. I'll get him."

Miller changed his position, orienting himself towards the bulk of the *Event Horizon*. Taking a deep breath and cursing his fortunes in this world, he kicked off.

He was not about to lose anyone, not now, not on this mission.

Not Justin.

Starck worked frantically at the airlock control panel, trying everything she could think of, short of hammering on the panel with her fist. There was no response at all from the panel.

"He's engaged the override," she said, stepping back. Frustrated, she smacked her hand against the control panel.

"Can you shut it down?" Peters asked.

"I'll try," Starck said. She turned, took a step, went to work on the access panel for the airlock. She had it open in a matter of moments, digging into the circuitry. All she needed was some way to screw up the outer door mechanism. If she could stop the outer door cycle, they could take their time getting the inner door open again.

DJ was peering at Justin through the hatch window. Turning to Peters, he said, "He's in some kind of trance. Try and make eye contact, talk him down. I'll be right back."

DJ turned and ran out of the airlock bay.

Peters started hammering on the hatch, trying to snap Justin out of his trance, or to at least get his attention. "Justin!" she screamed, her throat feeling like liquid fire. "Open the door! Open the door!"

Justin's expression did not change and he did not look at her. He reached out again, slowly, touching the control panel inside the airlock. He started to move, slowly, drifting sideways and up. He had executed a localized shutdown of the artificial gravity, a utility function that had been intended to help transition delicate cargo between zero-g and local gravity.

Justin looked like a man lost in a dream.

Coming to him, Starck," Miller said, wishing he had a full EVA thruster pack on his suit. "Gimme status."

He was using the *Event Horizon* as a means of propulsion, shoving himself from section to section. The huge ship was blurring by beneath him as he gained more and more velocity. He was going to have to shed some of that and change vectors sooner or later, and that was going to hurt.

"You better hurry," Starck said, her voice urgent. "He's engaged the override and we can't open the inner door."

Miller swore, pushed himself onward.

Peters was still hammering at the door, her hand hurting. "The door, Justin! Open the door!" She coughed, the effort of so much yelling taking its toll on her.

Justin turned slowly around, to stare at the outer door of the airlock. There was nothing on the other side of that door but space.

"Did you hear it?" Justin said, suddenly, his voice carried through the airlock intercom. His voice was flat, the voice of someone dead.

The hair stood up on the back of Peters' neck. Starck came over to stand beside her, staring at Justin.

"Yes," she said, willing to lie, to do anything if it would save Justin. "Yes, Justin, we heard it."

"Keep him talking," Starck whispered.

Peters nodded, sharply. "Do you know what it was?"

"It gets inside you," Justin said, softly. There was no

tension in his body. He hung in the microgravity like a mannequin. "It shows you things . . . horrible things . . ." A shuddering breath, almost a sob. "Can't describe it . . . there are no words. . . ."

Weir, on the bridge, had moved to the communications workstation, sitting unmoving. The intraship intercom system was open, tied into the radio. He had not missed a moment of the conversation.

He sat rigid, listening, trying to keep his mind blank and empty.

"What, Justin?" Peters was saying. "What shows you?"

Then Justin, almost crying: "It won't stop, it goes on and on and on. . . ."

"What does?" Peters said.

Weir closed his eyes.

"The dark inside me," Justin said.

Weir moaned. The tension went out of him. He leaned forward onto the console, his head in his hands.

The darkness was coming.

Miller's breath was coming in hard ragged gasps now as he made his way along the hull of the *Event Horizon*. He had made one vector change already, and had the aching arms to show for it.

He sailed onward.

"It's inside and it eats and eats until there's nothing left," Justin was moaning.

" 'The dark inside'?" Peters said, her voice sounding remarkably calm. "I don't understand."

"From the Other Place," Justin said.

Miller passed from shadow to light and back to shadow. Neptune turned beneath him, the Great Dark Spot malevolent at the edge of his vision.

The other crew," Justin said, softly. He lifted an arm, the movement causing him to turn slowly in the microgravity. "They're there, they're waiting for me. They're waiting for you. I won't go back there . . . I won't. . . ."

Peters pressed up against the airlock door, trying to keep her expression calm. There had to be some way to break through to Justin, some way to make him continue to find his way out of this fugue or whatever it was that had overcome him.

"Justin," she said, using her best motherly voice, the one that worked so well with Denny, "look at me. Look at me. Open this door."

DJ was back, sprinting into the bay, his medkit in hand. He almost slammed into the airlock, gasping for breath.

Starck said, urgently, "I don't think she can talk him down."

DJ looked at Justin, gently floating in the airlock, then at Starck. He stepped away from the airlock. "If he opens the outer door he'll turn inside-out."

Peters was watching Justin, trying to marshal her thoughts. Starck was still trying to do something with the airlock control circuit, her hands lost in a jumble of wiring and circuit modules, her face beading with sweat.

"Almost got it," Starck muttered.

"Come on, Baby Bear," Peters said, "open this door."

Justin was staring at her now, his eyes devoid of spirit. She could not imagine what he might have experienced in the heart of the Core. Justin had been changed, stripped of himself.

He raised a hand, touching the hatch window. "If you could see the things I've seen, you wouldn't try to stop me."

"That's not you talking," Peters said, her heart breaking. "Come back to us. Come back to me, Baby Bear."

Hope surged in her as Justin's hand moved, floating toward the switch that would open the inner airlock door. She tried to will him to make the final motion, throw the switch, open the door, get this nightmare ended.

His hand moved again, stabbing at the outer door control.

"*Noooo!*" Peters screamed.

Warning lights flashed on, inside and outside of the airlock. A Klaxon honked warning, reverberant, even louder inside the airlock than outside in the bay. Justin covered his ears with his hands, squeezed his eyes shut.

From somewhere, a computer voice, all modulated reason and no humanity: "Stand by for decompression. Thirty seconds."

Inside the airlock, Justin opened his eyes, staring. Peters gasped. Justin's eyes were clear, alive. Whatever had taken hold of him had been shaken off, at least for now.

He reached out with one hand, making his motion worse. "Hey . . ." he said, slowly, sounding confused, "what are you doing?" He turned his head wildly, making his spinning motion worse. Peters could see the realization strike. "Oh my God. *Oh my God!*" He lunged for the hatch.

Peters whirled. "Starck!"

Starck pulled back from the airlock access compartment, her expression horrified. "I can't! The inner door can't open once the outer door has been triggered. It would decompress the entire ship."

The computer continued to count down, heedless of human dilemmas.

Justin screamed, "Get me outta here!" He swung a fist at the door, but all it did was make him bounce. "If that door opens, I'm gonna—*oh God, my eyes!*"

Peters was losing her battle against hysteria, hanging on grimly. "We have to do something . . . oh God . . ."

Counting down.

Miller caromed from one piece of superstructure to another, hurtling through space in a dizzying, sickening parabola, kicking off again.

"Captain," Starck said, "Justin just activated the door. It's on a thirty-second delay."

"Patch me through to him," Miller said.

Kicking off again, hurtling along the endless *Event Horizon*. Nothing compressed about this ship, and never mind the origins of its name or its main drive unit.

He could hear the computer counting down.

"Justin," Miller said, his tone firm, authoritative.

"Skipper," Justin gasped out, "help me, help . . . tell them to let me in!"

Brusquely, Miller said, "They can't do that, Justin. Now listen carefully—"

Miller came over the edge of the ship, caught himself on an antenna, swung over. The muscles in his right arm protested at the brutal misuse.

He kicked off again.

There. He could see the bulge of the airlock.

"I don't want to die!" Justin screamed.

"You're not going to die!" Miller snapped. He kicked, flew on. "Not today! I want you to do exactly as I say and I'm gonna get you out of there, all right?"

And I hope like hell that I'm not bullshitting you, man.

There was a low thump as the air pumps started. Justin looked up, and around as air moved by him. The airlock was being evacuated rapidly.

"Oh God, it's starting," he cried.

"Justin," Miller said, his voice coming from the intercom speaker overhead, getting thinner, "I won't let you die."

Justin was crying helplessly, the dark and the cold pressing in on him. His tears flowed from his face, hung in the air. "Help me," he whispered.

He started to hyperventilate, trying to hold on to as much oxygen as he could.

"Tuck yourself into a crouched position," Miller said. His voice had a father's authority, and Justin tried to obey it, hurrying, pushing against the wall and huddling into a corner.

His tears were turning to blood as the pressure dropped.

"My eyes," Justin muttered. It felt as though someone was trying to push them from their sockets. He moaned with the pain.

"Shut 'em," Miller yelled, his voice fading as the air went away. "Shut your eyes, tight as you can!"

"Five seconds," Starck said, her voice sounding muffled.

There was a low booming sound, as though something had hit the superstructure near the airlock.

"Exhale everything you've got, Justin," Miller was yelling. "We can't have any air in those lungs, blow it all out!"

Justin had squeezed his eyes shut, clamping his hands over them. He could feel the blood, slick, sticky, too much of it, far too much of it.

"Oh God, oh God," he whimpered. He was going to die, he knew he was going to die. The darkness would have him, the voice would have him.

Somewhere in the distance, the last fading sound of Miller's voice. "Now, Mr. Justin! *Do it!*"

Justin breathed out, hard, everything gone in one last spasmodic moment, one last silent scream.

The outer door slid open.

Chapter Thirty-four

It was a matter of timing now.

Miller hunched down, watching the airlock, his concentration becoming absolute. He had about five meters to cross, he estimated.

The airlock opened.

There was a puff of vapor as the last of the atmosphere blew out, carrying Justin with it. The engineer was curled up into a ball, his arms wrapped around his knees.

Miller sprang up and outwards, pushing as hard as he could, grunting with the effort. He spread his arms as he leapt outward, seeing the brightness of Neptune.

He slammed into Justin, tumbling them both back toward the ship. There was more pain as he struck the side of the airlock, but he disregarded it, turning himself, holding Justin with one hand while he used the other to pull them both into the open airlock, keeping one boot pressed up against the side of the airlock in case the door decided to try and close on them.

They tumbled inside.

Miller reached out and slapped the switch that closed the

outer door, going more by gut instinct that anything else. The door closed, too slowly for his taste.

Justin floated in the middle of the compartment, his veins bulging, pinkish ice covering his skin, his face covered with a layer of frozen blood that had streamed from his mouth, nose and eyes. Capillaries had burst everywhere in his face and hands, very likely in other places too. If he survived this experience, Justin would spend some time looking like a road map of hell.

The outer door locked.

The count in Miller's head told him five seconds had elapsed since the door had opened.

The airlock began to repressurize quickly. That might do more damage to Justin, but that was a chance they had to take. Miller despised the lack of options, but he was not about to abandon hope.

He reached out again and slapped the control that triggered the artificial gravity, cradling Justin as he slowly dropped to the deck. Through the window in the hatch he could see the anxious faces of Peters, Starck and DJ.

A green light. Miller reached out, hit the switch to open the inner door, then flattened against the wall as Peters and DJ rushed in.

"Oh God, Justin . . ." Peters said.

DJ went to one knee, his medkit open already. Peters knelt on the other side, taking Justin's wrist. DJ got Justin's mouth open, slipped in a tube. There was the hiss of oxygen.

"I've got a pulse," Peters said. "He's alive." She reached out, pulled an instrument from DJ's medkit, unrolling a blood pressure cuff, slipping it over Justin's bicep.

"Pressure?" DJ said.

Peters looked terrified. "Forty over twenty and falling."

"He's crashing," DJ said, flatly.

Blood suddenly bubbled from Justin's mouth and nose. He gasped desperately, choked, and then screamed hoarsely. Blood sprayed the airlock, spattered DJ, Peters, Miller.

"He can breathe," DJ said, his tone ironic. "That's good. Let's get him to Medical, go, go!"

All three of them bent to pick up Justin, Miller not even stopping to get his helmet off.

Chapter Thirty-five

Weir sat at the gravity drive console on the bridge, listening to voices in the air and watching a phantom spin on the display in front of him. He had tried to watch Neptune, but he could not focus on the planet for very long. He could have turned his attention to scanning for the rings of debris, or trying to locate the Neptunian moons, but he had no heart for that.

Voices in the air.

DJ saying, "Intubate, pure oxygen feed, get the nitrogen out of his blood."

Then Peters, almost frantic: "His peritoneum has ruptured."

Miller had managed quite a rescue, it seemed, but that was what he was good at.

It was too late, Weir thought, too late in the day. He doubted that Miller was as brilliant a rescuer as they would all need. They were drowning and no one realized it.

DJ again: "One thing at a time, let's keep him breathing. Start the drip, 15ccs fibrinogen . . ."

The computer model of the gateway swelled on the display

before him, rendered out now, showing the hotspots and the magnetic flow. It was a live thing, breathing energy in and out, flowing from the Core at the heart of the ship.

I am Death, the Destroyer of Worlds. J. Robert Oppenheimer, quoting the Bhagavad Gita, dismayed by the explosion of one tiny atomic device . . . what would he have said to a power source that involved the inescapable energies of a collapsed star? *The physicists have known sin*, Oppenheimer had said later, only to be pilloried by a world that wanted the destructive forces without the moral boundaries.

Peters, frightened but holding that professional edge: "Christ, he's bleeding out, pressure's still dropping . . . he's going into arrhythmia—"

They were losing one. In times past, everyone had been lost, all hands down with the ship. What was the point of fighting back, fighting to survive? The darkness swallowed everyone eventually, no matter how much they might be loved, no matter how valuable they were. In the end, the only way to deal with the darkness was on its own terms, at a dead run, giving in to that one last plunge into the unknown.

DJ, urgent: "We have to defib . . . *clear!*"

The bang of the defibrillator, the sound of a body convulsing under the power of electricity. In the end, medicine had not progressed far. The galvanic force was as much a going concern now as it had been when Mary Wollstonecraft Shelley had written *Frankenstein*. He with the most electronvolts wins the game.

The diagram drew him in, seeping into the empty places where his soul had once lived. A live thing, it shifted before his eyes, compelling.

Gently, a lover's caress, he touched a switch. He felt the surge of power, the changes within the heart of the ship.

The screen cleared. Pristine text flashed up in place of the embedding diagram: *Commencing gravity drive initialization process. Gravity drive will be primed for ignition in two hours.*

Chapter Thirty-six

Cooper and Smith had remained outside, working as fast as possible on the *Lewis and Clark*. The rest, Weir included, had congregated in the Gravity Couch Bay of the *Event Horizon*. DJ and Peters had managed to save Justin in the finish, but it had been close.

Miller was more exhausted than he had ever been in his life.

Justin was now floating in one of the Gravity Couches, suspended in a bilious green gel. He had become a patchwork man, his body damaged as much by the work that had saved him as by the original trauma.

"We were able to stabilize him," DJ was saying, "enough to get him into a tank. He'll live, if we ever make it back."

"We'll make it," Miller said, firmly. "Good work." He looked at Starck. "How long?"

"CO_2 levels will become toxic in four hours," Starck said. She looked as though she was ready to fall down at any second. He figured they all were in shock over Justin . . . except for Weir. Weir seemed incapable of that sort of emotional investment.

Peters was standing in front of Justin's Gravity Couch, her face a mask of grief. Almost losing Justin was as bad for her as almost losing her son.

Miller walked over to her, slowly, hating to do this to her now, hating the fact that he could not avoid it. If they were to survive, he needed everything he could possibly accumulate.

"Peters," he said, keeping his voice gentle, soft. She looked around at him, her eyes big, red-rimmed, still close to tears. Medical detachment could go only so far, he realized. "We need to know what happened to the last crew. Before it happens to us."

"I'll get back to the log," she said, her voice weak. She looked away from him, off into her own personal distance. She was getting the thousand-meter stare. "But on the bridge. I won't go back into Medical."

"Fine," Miller said.

Peters walked away from him, leaving the Gravity Couch Bay. He wished there was something he could do for her. At the moment he was not certain that he could do anything for any of them.

Weir watched Peters leave, wondering what mission Miller had sent her on this time. He knew she had been very attached to Justin, had tended to mother the crew. It must be very difficult for her right now.

Starck, standing next to him, said, "Justin said something about 'the dark inside me.' What does that mean?"

Weir looked up at the tank. Justin had been interesting to contemplate from an engineering point of view, just in terms of how much damage a human body could sustain and still keep on functioning.

It was not Justin in the tank.

It was Claire, his wife. She was naked, her hair streaming around her face, dark trails flowing from her hands.

He stared, perplexed.

Without thinking, he said, "I don't think it means anything."

He blinked.

Justin floated in the Gravity Couch, unmoving.

"You weren't there," Starck said.

Miller had walked over to them. Weir looked at him, suddenly uncomfortable.

"That's right," Miller said, looking down at Weir, unwavering. "Where were you?"

"I was on the bridge," Weir said. The truth, the whole truth, and nothing but the truth.

Without waiting for an answer, Weir turned and walked out of the Gravity Couch Bay. He could be useful on the bridge while the minutes ticked away.

He heard footsteps behind him, following down the corridor. Angry, he turned around. Miller almost ran into him.

"I want to know what caused that noise," Miller said, his tone dark, almost threatening. "I want to know why one of my crew tried to throw himself out of the airlock."

Weir sighed. "Thermal changes in the hull could have caused the metal to expand and contract very suddenly, causing reverberations—"

"That's *bullshit* and *you* know it!" Miller shouted. He waved a finger under Weir's nose, making the scientist step back. "You built this fucking ship and all I've heard from you is *bullshit!*"

"What do you want me to say?" Weir muttered darkly.

Miller contained himself with an effort. "You said this ship's drive creates a gateway."

"Yes," Weir said, trying to keep his patience.

"To what? Where did this ship go? Where did you send it?"

"I don't know," Weir said. It was interesting how disarming honesty could be, considering the circumstances.

"Where has it been for the past seven years?" Miller said, his tone darkening.

If I had that answer, we would have been here a lot sooner, Weir thought. "I don't know."

Miller was losing his temper again. " 'I don't know?' You're supposed to be the expert, and the only answer I've had from you is 'I don't know.' " Miller grimaced, a man trying desperately to get blood from a stone. "The 'Other Place,' what is that?"

"*I don't know!*" Weir yelled, taking a step toward Miller. This time it was the Captain's turn to step back. Weir got himself under control, breathing deeply of the foul air. "I don't know. There's a lot of things going on here that I don't understand. Truth takes time."

"That's exactly what we don't have, Doctor," Miller said, and he brushed past Weir, heading off down the corridor toward the bridge.

Weir watched him walk away.

Chapter Thirty-seven

Miller stalked through the corridors, taking the long way around to the bridge, trying to shake off the residue of anger that lingered after his attempt to get answers from Weir. He had been furious enough to want to smack Weir silly, but had known better than to let fly. They might yet need the scientist.

Jesus Christ, Miller thought, stalking, *does he have to be so goddamned* useless?

There was more there, though, something he had yet to put his finger on. Weir had changed somehow, his attitude altering, hardening. Weir was a case and a half in himself.

He reached a junction, made a left turn.

"Don't leave me!"

The voice echoed along the corridors from somewhere in the distance. Miller turned, his skin crawling, trying to figure out the direction it had come from.

"Where are you?" he shouted.

His voice reverberated in the corridors, but the echoes were the only answer he received. He stepped backward, turning, stumbled over sections of piping on the floor.

"What do you want?" he shouted.

"Oh God, please help me!" A hollow voice, dead for these years, screaming out a plea across time.

Miller bent down, scooping up a short section of pipe, driven more by instinct than anything else. "Get out of my fucking head!" he screamed.

He hurled the pipe down the corridor he was facing, heard it clang as it hit, clattering as it bounced and rolled away.

Silence. There was an emptiness in his head now.

Miller turned, his back against the corridor wall. He felt weak, weary. Slowly, he slid down until he was sitting. He hunched up, putting his head in his hands, fighting the tears, the memories, the shame.

Corrick . . .

Chapter Thirty-eight

The Gravity Couch Bay was deserted now, except for Justin floating in his tank. DJ walked in, went over to the tank, checked the readouts. They were going to have to figure out how to transfer Justin to the *Lewis and Clark* eventually. Miller was not planning to try to retrieve the *Event Horizon*.

"Any change?" Miller said.

DJ whirled around, surprised. Miller smiled. DJ was tough to rattle. Miller, however, had been sitting quietly in deep shadows, trying to marshal his thoughts so he could get on with the job, whatever the job had turned into.

DJ walked toward him. "No, no change," he said. There was a long pause. Something was troubling DJ. "I've analyzed his blood samples. There's no evidence of excessive levels of carbon dioxide. Or anything else out of the ordinary."

Miller laughed, a cold, grim sound that he knew would transmit to DJ the depths of the defeat he felt. "Of course not. He just climbed into the airlock because he felt like it. Just one of those things." Miller straightened up, angrily pushing against the hopelessness. "We almost lost him today. I will not lose another man."

DJ raised an eyebrow, watching Miller carefully. "Another man?"

Miller nodded. He unzipped his flight suit slightly, reached inside, pulled out a small service medal, showed it to DJ. He had kept it with him since it had been awarded to him in a service essentially devoid of pomp and circumstance. It served as a reminder.

"Edmund Corrick," Miller said, softly. The memories flooded in again, just as they had in the corridor. "Young guy, a lot like Justin. He was with me on the *Goliath*." A laughing face, a smart-ass kid on the way to making a name for himself in the service, a bit on the skinny side. Miller had considered the kid a bit of a geek, but he liked him anyway. "Four of us had made it to the lifeboat. Corrick was still on board when the fire . . ."

Roaring around corners, across the deck, the bulkheads, the ceiling, a living thing that melted metal and sang with a monster's voice . . .

DJ waited, silent.

"Have you ever seen fire in zero gravity?" Miller went on, suddenly. "It's like a liquid, it slides over everything. Corrick saw the fire and froze. Just stood there screaming." Miller swallowed, remembering, his chest hollow. "Screaming for me to save him."

"What did you do?"

Miller was silent, staring.

Corrick, burning, screaming. It had been an oxygen fire. Fast and hot, from nothing to destruction in the time it took to draw a breath. Had the circumstances been slightly different, there would have been no survivors of the *Goliath*.

Miller tried to get the words out, but it was hard, almost impossible. He had lived with this for too many years now, had thought he had the grief and rage stored away somewhere else.

He pushed against his block, determined. The truth needed to be told. "The only thing I could do," he said, finally, letting the images play. "I shut the lifeboat hatch. I left him behind. And then the fire hit him . . . and he was gone."

Crawling up Corrick's legs, along his arms, dripping over him like hot white rain. . . .

He could not have gone back. Those in the lifeboat would have died along with Corrick. The Board of Inquiry had commended Miller for his forthright actions in saving the others. He did not tell them the complete circumstances of Corrick's death.

He had always wondered if he should have gone back, tried to retrieve Corrick. He knew that they would both have died, but it did not remove the guilt.

"You never told me," DJ said.

"I never told anyone until now," Miller said, softly. "But this ship knew, DJ. It knows about the *Goliath*, it knows about Corrick. It knows our secrets. It knows what we're afraid of. It's in all our heads, and I don't know how long I can fight it." Miller slumped, frustrated, not knowing what sort of sense he was making, if any. "Go ahead, say it. I'm losing my fucking mind."

DJ continued watching Miller, his gaze unshakable. *Damn you*, Miller thought, *you should be a shrink, not a trauma doc.* "Maybe," DJ said, "maybe not."

DJ's tone pulled Miller out of his misery for a moment, gave him the suggestion of hope. "You know something."

DJ licked his lips. He nodded towards the Gravity Couch Bay workstation. "I've . . . I've been listening to the transmission again." DJ walked toward the workstation. Miller stood up and followed him. "And I think I made a mistake in the translation."

"Go on," Miller said.

DJ tapped in commands, pulling up the filtered version of the recording USAC had picked up. Partway through it, as Miller's nerves were jangling from the unholy racket, DJ stopped the playback.

"I thought it said 'liberate me,' " DJ said slowly. " 'Save me.' But it's not 'me' . . . it's 'liberate Tu-temet.' " DJ glanced down at the console, up at Miller. " 'Save yourself.' "

Miller tried to untense, but he could not. "It's not a distress call. It's a warning."

"It gets worse," DJ said. Miller stared at him, saying nothing. How much worse could it get? "It's very hard to make out, but listen to this final part." DJ started the recording again, and Miller's nerves tightened another notch. If they made it out of here, he was going to have nightmares for years to come. "Do you hear it? Right there."

"Hear what?"

"The final words." DJ hesitated for a moment, then plunged on. "They sound like 'ex inferis.' *Inferis*, the ablative case of *inferi*. 'From Hell.' "

" 'Save yourself from Hell.' " Miller shook his head, trying to work all of this into something coherent. "Starck's telling me this ship is alive, now you're saying . . . what are you saying? This ship is possessed?"

DJ was shaking his head. "No. I don't . . . I can't believe in that sort of thing." He glanced at the workstation again. "But if Weir is right, this ship has passed beyond our universe, beyond reality. Who knows where it's been . . . what it's seen." He looked at Miller, his expression wavering, his mask starting to slip away. "And what it's brought back with it."

Miller had no answer for this and could find nothing to say that would make any sense. The things that had happened aboard the *Event Horizon* defied reason.

The intercom hissed as the circuit opened. Both Miller and DJ whirled at the sound.

"Captain Miller?" It was Cooper.

"Better be good news, Cooper," Miller said.

"Yes, sir," Cooper replied. There was a jovial tone to his voice. "We are ready to repressurize the *Clark* and get the hell out of here."

Miller could have kissed him.

Chapter Thirty-nine

Cooper and Smith remained on station on the hull of the *Lewis and Clark*, keeping an eye on their patches. Miller suited up again and went down though the umbilicus, into the ship, heading for the bridge. All of the systems had been powered down, conserving energy until the repairs were complete.

Time to get on with it, Miller thought. He reached out and turned a manual valve, opening the surviving atmospheric tanks.

"All right, Cooper," he said.

"Cross your fingers," Cooper said, but Miller knew that was intended for Smith's benefit.

Air arrived as a thin mist at first, fading away as the pressure increased and the air warmed up. Miller stood stock-still, watching the readout for the EVA suit's exterior pressure sensor.

"It's holding," Smith said. "She's holding!"

Calmly, a counterpoint to Smith's excitement, Cooper said, "We're still venting trace gasses. Gimme about twenty minutes to plug the hole."

"You're a lifesaver, Coop," Miller said. Relief flooded him. "Twenty minutes."

"Twenty minutes," he heard Smith say. "We're going home."

"About goddamn time," Cooper said.

Miller smiled, undogged his helmet, lifting it off. He took a deep breath. The air had a slight metallic tang to it, but it was nectar compared to the state of the *Event Horizon*'s air.

"Back in business," Miller said to himself.

His ship. His rules.

The *Event Horizon* could go to hell.

Chapter Forty

They were running out of time and she was getting no-where.

Peters frowned angrily at the sciences workstation display, tempted to smack the thing with her fist to see if that would achieve anything. The log was stubbornly refusing to resolve into anything useful. She was tired and she hated spending her time doing this—she just wanted to get out of here and go home.

She might even resign from USAC, try and make her way as an groundhog. Denny needed her.

Rapidly, she typed in another set of instructions and smacked the enter key with more force than necessary. She stood up, stretched, not that this helped her aching back in any way, and turned to Starck, who was busy at the other side of the bridge.

"You got any coffee?" Peters said.

Starck looked around, nodded. "It's cold."

"I don't care," she said.

She went over to Starck, picked up a mug, filled it half-way. If it was intolerable, she could probably find some way of warming it up. The bridge had to have a microwave, she figured, considering how much other stuff had been crammed into it.

She turned back to her workstation. To her surprise, something was actually happening with the log video. The computer was finally managing to break through the signal noise, making something of the recording.

The process was rapid now. Colors blurred, changed, solidified. Images began to form. There was movement. There was . . .

Peters felt numb, boneless. The coffee mug slipped from her fingers, shattering on the deck, coffee spilling over her boots.

"Starck," she whispered.

Starck turned, left her seat, stood by Peters, staring. "Sweet Jesus," she said, her voice hushed. She turned again, got to the intercom. "Miller . . . *Miller!*"

Peters somehow found a seat, sat down heavily, stared out of the bridge windows at Neptune. She tried to empty her mind and wash away the things she had seen, but she knew that would be impossible.

She closed her eyes. Tears streamed down her face.

Miller stood behind Starck, watching the screen.

Starck had not been particularly coherent in her message to him, but she had somehow managed to get the point across—Peters had managed to clear up the scrambled log entry.

Weir and DJ had arrived just after him and now stood to either side of him. Peters was sitting in another bridge seat, not looking at the screen. She could not bear seeing the log playback.

He could not believe what he was seeing, did not know quite how to react to it, other than with disgust and horror.

The image on the display was flickering and rolling still, despite the best efforts of the software. As far as Miller was concerned, it was too clear.

There were four of the *Event Horizon*'s crew in the image, including Captain Kilpack. To one side of Kilpack, a crew member was somehow contorting himself impossibly, his right arm twisted, his head tilting back. His features were unrecognizable.

Starck blanched and looked away.

Continuing the impossible motions, the man shoved his hand into his mouth. There was a distant wet sound. Miller could see the man's shoulder loosening, dislocating.

There was blood everywhere in the image. So much blood.

Beyond Kilpack, a man and a woman were engaged in frantic sex, she wrapped around him as he rammed himself into her. Both of them were covered in blood. She had dug her fingernails into his back, tearing into the flesh, leaving gory tears that streamed blood down his back, though he seemed oblivious to either pain or injury.

The other man had now forced a good part of his arm down his throat. More blood there, streaming out from his mouth, from his nose.

Kilpack turned, smiling.

The woman turned her head, opening her mouth. In a blur of motion, she drove her face into her partner's neck, biting down, tearing. A chunk of bleeding flesh fell and struck the deck. Blood pumped freely, spraying her, drenching his shoulder, pouring down his arm. She drove into the wound again, heedless of the blood, tearing the wound wider. His head lolled to one side, loose in death. Yet he did not cease his maniacal thrusting.

Miller wanted to turn away, to shut off the playback, to end it now, but he had to know, had to see it all if he had any hope of ever understanding what had happened here.

The man with his arm down his own throat had continued his contortions. Miller, sickened, could not imagine what he was trying to achieve, what he was being driven to.

The question was answered a few moments later.

With soft, glutinous sounds, the man withdrew his arm. Blood bubbled up, a torrent of it. He had grasped a handful of his innards, pulling them up, releasing them to fall wetly at his feet while he swayed, dripping blood and flesh, dead eyes staring into the distance.

The woman bit again and again as her dead partner continued his thrusting. She made no move to release him or push him away.

Kilpack turned.

Full fathom five thy father lies, Miller remembered, Shakespeare from high school or perhaps later, *The Tempest* coming to mind as Kilpack held out his hands, *those are pearls that were his eyes.* . . .

In the palms of Kilpack's hands, nestled in blood, were his eyes, held out now like an offering. Where his eyes had been were empty sockets, lined with torn flesh. Blood oozed down over his cheeks, around his mouth, over his chin.

Kilpack opened his mouth slowly, seeming almost exultant. His lips moved, forming words. In a deep, strange voice that was nothing like the one Miller had heard on the earlier log entries, Kilpack said, "*Liberate tu-Temet ex inferis.* . . . "

Miller could take no more. He reached out, slapping the workstation, shutting the video playback off.

There was silence on the bridge.

"We're leaving," Miller said, his voice flat.

Weir stepped in front of him, determined. "We can't leave. Our orders are specific—"

"To rescue the crew and salvage the ship," Miller said, wishing Weir would get the hell out of his face, the hell out of his way, maybe just cease to be. "The crew is dead, Dr. Weir. This ship killed them."

Weir was not about to be put off. "We came here to do a job."

"We are aborting, Dr. Weir," Miller said, as coldly as he could. Weir had watched the log playback and he could still beg for the life of this evil ship? "Take one last look around."

Ignoring Weir, he turned to the others. "Starck, download all the files from the *Event Horizon*'s computers. DJ, get Justin transferred to the *Clark*—"

"We'll have to move the tank," DJ said.

"Then move the tank." DJ nodded and left the bridge, moving fast. "Peters, get the CO_2 scrubbers back into the *Clark*."

Weir was in his face again, his expression agonized. "Don't do this."

"It's done," Miller snapped.

He turned and walked off the bridge.

Chapter Forty-one

Weir had a death wish, Miller was sure of it. The scientist just could not let things be, would not let go and get on with his life. Now he was coming after Miller again, chasing him down the corridor.

Miller let Weir catch up, then turned, staring at him.

Without missing a beat, Weir snapped, "What about my ship? We can't just leave her—"

"I have no intention of leaving her," Miller said, using the coldest, angriest voice he could summon up. It was a voice that could cow any crew member foolish enough to cause it to be summoned. Weir didn't even flinch. "I will take the *Lewis and Clark* to a safe distance and then launch tac missiles at the *Event Horizon* until I am satisfied that she has been vaporized." He glared at Weir for a long moment. "Fuck this ship."

"You can't just destroy her!" Weir cried.

"Watch me," Miller said, and he turned away from Weir, hoping that this would be the end of it, knowing it was not.

Weir lunged at Miller, grabbing hold of his flight suit and turning him around abruptly. The scientist had a savagely angry look to him. Miller lifted his arms, breaking Weir's hold on him, slamming the scientist back into the bulkhead, leaning over him.

Once again, Weir was not cowed. He stared at Miller, challenging, angry, willing to fight. Miller raised a fist, willing to end it there and then, even if it meant having to patch Weir up and ship him back under medical conditions. So it would be one more thing to try and explain to Hollis. . . .

The lights went out. After a very brief pause, the emergency lighting flickered on, turning the corridor into a place of shadows.

"Miller, come in," Starck, over the intercom, aggravated.

Miller lowered his fist and pushed Weir away from him, backing away until he found the nearest intercom panel. "Starck, what the hell is going on?"

"We lost main power again," Starck said. More than aggravation now. There was fear and anger in her voice. She knew as well as he did that these power losses were nothing to do with the state of the *Event Horizon*.

Weir was barely visible in the darkness now, though Miller could see his eyes well enough. Focused, burning with hatred.

"Goddammit!" Miller snapped, more at Weir than at Starck. "Starck, get those files and vacate. I want off this ship."

He backed away from the intercom.

Weir was moving back into the shadows now, even his eyes fading into the gloom. Miller hated the lunatic design of this ship, hated the flying buttresses and faux-Gothic arches, casting pools of darkness everywhere under the emergency lighting.

"You can't leave," Weir whispered, echoing in the darkness. "She won't let you."

Miller walked toward the scientist, but he was having trouble seeing him now. "Just get your gear back onto the *Lewis and Clark*, Doctor, or you'll find yourself looking for a ride home."

Weir was gone, like smoke in a breeze, vanished in the darkness. Inwardly Miller raged, wondering how Weir could pull a stunt like this, could get away from him.

"I am home," Weir whispered, but it seemed as though the voice came from all around him now.

The main lights suddenly flared up, drenching the corridor in halogen brightness. Miller ran forward, stopped, looking around. Weir was nowhere in sight. He might as well have never been there.

"Weir?" he called. *"Weir!"*

No answer but echoes.

He went back to the intercom, slammed the side of his fist into it, not caring if he broke it. "All hands. Dr. Weir is missing. I want him found and contained."

He set off jogging in the direction he had last seen Weir, not expecting to find the scientist, intending mayhem if he did.

Chapter Forty-two

Smith had joined Peters on the *Event Horizon*, racing through the ship to retrieve all of the CO_2 scrubbers they had used to try keeping the air somehow breathable. They would still be useful on the *Lewis and Clark*, giving them enough time to get started on the voyage back home and to get help once they were close to Daylight Station.

They worked their way steadily down into the Second Containment, both frustrated at the distribution of the cylinders, both aware that they would need almost every one of them. Spacecraft designers had not progressed far beyond the Apollo days when it came to processing atmosphere.

Smith was yanking cylinders out of a wall compartment while Peters went down to retrieve the last of them. Perversely enough, the scrubber compartment had been placed directly under the Core.

"Let's go, let's go," Smith was saying, pulling a last cylinder out, getting it boxed. "This place freaks me out."

"You want to suffocate on the ride home?" Peters called up to him. She ducked down, calling up to him, "Last one!"

The cylinder was stubborn, refusing to come out as easily as it had gone in.

"Come on," Smith called.

"Goddammit!" Peters growled, hauling back. The cylinder slipped free suddenly, offbalancing her. She lost her grip on the scrubber, missing it as it fell into the coolant around her feet, disappearing from sight. "Shit!"

"Leave it," Smith called down. "We don't have time, let's go!"

The hell with it. She bent down and fished around, getting hold of the end of the cylinder, pulling it free of the muck. Not wasting time in gloating to Smith, she turned around and got back up to the storage boxes, packing the slick cylinder away. Smith had lost a cylinder in the sludge himself, but they could manage without it.

They finished packing up as quickly as they could, each taking a case of the scrubbers and heading out of the Second Containment and into the corridor. The case was heavy, and Peters found herself falling behind Smith, who loped ahead like a man possessed. She decided she was not going to worry about it—Smith was halfway to crazy anyway, and only Miller was capable of keeping up with the man.

She took a deep breath, praying that their ordeal would be over soon.

There was a giggle behind her, childlike, echoing.

She stopped, shocked. Her heart pounded.

In a whisper, she said, "Denny?" She turned back to look down to the Second Containment. She could still see the Core from here, a dark shape within the darkness. There was nothing else to see.

She started to turn back, aware that she had lost sight of Smith.

At the corner of her vision, she saw a swift movement, a tiny figure that dashed across the Second Containment's outer area. It couldn't be. . . .

"Denny?" she said again, her voice barely even a whisper. Her head was filling with fog again. Something was wrong here, she knew that. She turned back. "Smith?"

Smith was gone. He was more than likely halfway to the main airlock by now, unaware that she had stopped.

She had to know.

She put down the scrubber case and started back toward the Second Containment, looking from side to side. There was nothing to be seen.

Another giggle. There was the scrape of metal upon metal.

Peters crept forward, trying to see into the deep shadows. "Den . . . ?" she whispered.

There was an open access panel in the outer area of the Second Containment. Peters bent down, trying to see inside. It was dark in there, the length of the duct reflecting the little light that there was.

She tried to clear her mind. How could Denny have been brought here? Miller was right, she knew that. The ship used the dark corners to get at them, and here was hers, in the form of Denny. She had loved him always . . . and she had fled from him too, gone back to space when she should have stayed with him, stayed around to help him.

"Mommy . . ." A plaintive voice, so far away.

She had left him behind on Earth and this evil ship had somehow reached out and brought him here, into its dark heart.

She could not allow Denny to be taken by this monster. Her son deserved a better fate than this, a better existence than the one she had afforded him.

She climbed into the service duct, ducking her head. "Den . . . ?" she called.

She had to move along almost crab-fashion, but her determination made her quick. Weir had been stuck in one of these service ducts, she remembered, cramped down and in the dark when the lights had gone out. She wondered what he had seen.

She stopped at a junction, looking both ways before continuing. She wished, desperately, that she had thought to pick up a flashlight before coming in here. There was no way of knowing what else might be in here besides Denny. She had an involuntary flash of memory, the log playback cascading through her mind, and her stomach turned. She fought it down, kept going.

There was a whisper behind her that could have been Denny's voice. She turned around, seeing nothing. There was a sound behind her at the junction, something like running feet, and she turned back again.

Nothing.

This time the whisper was in front of her. She eased across the junction, looking to either side again.

"Denny?" she called, moving on. "Denny, come to Mommy."

She knew the ship could be playing a game with her, but she could not be certain of that. If it had somehow brought Denny here . . .

A child laughing, amused, echoing in the distance. She continued onward, trailing it. She came to a vertical shaft. The laughter echoed down the shaft now, clear and bright. She straightened up, looking up the shaft.

No choice. She began climbing the ladder, moving steadily up the shaft. The laughter was becoming clearer and clearer the higher she climbed.

"Hold on," she said, "Mommy's coming."

Her arms and legs ached beyond belief, but she would not let the pain stop her. Not now, not while she had a chance to save her son from the *Event Horizon*.

The shaft ended at a catwalk. She pulled herself up onto the icy metal and stood up, looking around. She had no idea where she was in the ship, hoping only that she could get back to the *Lewis and Clark* once she had retrieved Denny.

Great machinery rose on either side of her, humming with the ugly sound of harnessed energy. The machines were dark, shining dimly under low lighting. The catwalk wove between the machines, the end invisible in the gloom.

Ahead of her a small figure was running.

"Den?" she called.

The lights flickered, reddened. The low, angry hum of the machines deepened in tone, making her head hurt. She felt the sound in the pit of her stomach.

She ran forward, came to a junction, turned wildly around, searching.

Denny was standing a few feet away, barely visible in the dimming light.

"Denny?" she said.

He was *standing*.

"Mommy," he said.

The ship had brought him here, given him this. She no longer knew whether she should laugh or cry. All she wanted was to get him out of here, make him safe.

The lights flickered.

She eased ahead. "You can walk," she whispered, staring, "Denny, you can *walk* . . . oh, my baby . . ."

The tears were starting now. All she could think of was Denny, of getting him out. Another few steps and she could get him out.

"Wanna show you, Mommy," Denny said, holding out his arms to her, just like he had held his arms out at his birthday party, "wanna show you something—"

Another step and she could hold on to him.

The catwalk disappeared from beneath her. Screaming, she fell, plunging down. There was nothing to grab hold of, nothing to save her. She turned over in midair, seeing the darkness of the Core, then passing it, turning again.

She slammed into the deck in front of the Core, feeling her body bend and splinter, the pain terrible for a few moments before it faded into a general numbness. She could not move, could not feel anything. Her breath came raggedly, suffused with blood.

"Denny," she whispered. A pool of blood was spreading out from under her. Even if she was found now, she knew that nothing could be done for her. She had fallen too far, too hard, there was too much damage.

She wished she could move.

Twenty meters above her, she could see Denny looking down at her, clapping his hands.

He giggled.

Chapter Forty-three

My ship, Weir thought, walking through the darkness. *My rules.*

The *Event Horizon* had its hooks in his heart, he knew that. He refused to accept the possibility that his wishes could be irrational. Far from it, in fact: his desires were in accordance with those of USAC, to retrieve the ship and resolve the mystery.

Miller was a madman, driven by a terror of the dark. He had no way of knowing what had happened here, what that bizarre log entry meant. For all Miller knew, or could know, the log entry had been an elaborate fake, hidden behind a blind of signal noise. On the basis of this, Miller was willing to destroy the *Event Horizon*. Billions of dollars had gone into the project, along with millions of man-hours and astonishing amounts of resources.

He walked through the darkness of the First Containment, into the separator tube. The sections spun around him, their vibrations feeding through his body.

He had poured his life into this vessel, had dedicated the lives of many others to its development and construction. It would seem that the lives of its first crew had been sacrificed in the course of its maiden voyage, lost in the headlong rush of some kind of madness. The *Event Horizon* had been a story of blood and pain . . . *his* blood, *his* pain. Once she had vanished, he had been nothing, had had nothing.

Except Claire. Once she was gone, he had become a dead man, walking through the days. One day his body would have caught up with his mind and he would simply have stopped, shutting down like an obsolete piece of equipment. USAC had not been willing to fund another grand experiment in starflight, not without knowing just why the first one had culminated in tremendous and embarrassing failure without even basic telemetry to show for it.

He could not give them answers. They would not give him another chance. In the end it had been people like Jack Hollis who had kept him going.

The return of the *Event Horizon* had been his resurrection. He was not going to walk away and die again, spending his days as a zombie until his heart ceased beating.

He walked past an abandoned CO_2 scrubber case, incurious. Let Miller do what he would. . . .

He passed into the Second Containment, passing an open service duct, unable to recall if he had closed up the one he had been in. Perhaps not. It did not matter, anyway, not now. What mattered now was completing the jump, proving the point.

He walked down toward the Core.

He stopped, staring, his mind working without formulating anything.

"Oh no," whispered, dismayed. "Peters. . . ." Even in the gloom, he recognized her. She seemed to have fallen from a great height, considering the way her body was twisted. He looked up, seeing an open service access overhead, one that would have been accessible from the magnetic containment generator bay.

He went down to her, crouched down, tried to figure out what he should do. Her eyes were open, black as a result of the fall, and she was not breathing. There was a lot of blood, a lot of damage, and he doubted that she had lived long after the impact, if she had survived the fall at all.

Peters had been kind to him. He had no friends in this world, and he was always grateful for a little kindness here and there. She had shown him that.

He grieved for her son, back on Earth.

He stood up, looking down at Peters' body, wondering if he should report this immediately, or let it pass. Miller would blame him, either way.

"Billy," a familiar voice whispered.

Slowly, unwilling, he looked up.

Claire was standing before the Core, a pale reflection with eyes of milk. Her hair hung around her as though immersed in water. She was naked, water dripping from her, and she was radiant with cold.

Weir stared, his eyes widening.

Reality blinked and time turned upon its head.

She lay on the bed, sapped of energy, drained of vitality, unable to function any longer. She stared at the wall, she had stared at the wall for hours. He could have gotten her off the station if he had wanted, taken her down Skyhook One and into the real light of day. He was dead though, and he had no compassion for her condition because she could not have saved him from the doom imposed upon him.

Weir looked frantically around. They were back on Daylight Station, back in his past.

He turned back to her. "Claire," he said, but the reaction he had hoped for was not there. He walked toward the bed, toward her. "Claire, it's Billy. I'm home. . . ."

He reached out.

Reality blinked and there was the sound of water running.

He turned his head.

Claire stood in the bathroom, brushing her teeth with methodical strokes. He glanced back at the bed, but it was empty, unmade, unwashed. He had hardly been there, working himself into a stupor as he tried to solve the mystery of the *Event Horizon* without the resources he needed.

These were moments in time.

He could not change them. He knew that, knew all of the theoretical physics behind the laws of the immutability of time. He had bent space between his hands, but time had mastered him.

He walked toward her, reaching out.

"I know I wasn't there for you," he said softly, slowly, despising this sudden flood of platitudes, hating himself with each word, angry at a universe that could be so cruel as to do this to him. "I'm sorry. I let my work come between us, but I'm here now, I'm here. If you could just let me hold you. I've been—"

Reality blinked, sweeping away his words, his thoughts, sickening him in the transition. His pulse raced, and he felt the surge of adrenaline. Time was sliding beneath him, there was no time. . . .

Claire sat on the closed toilet, carefully shaving her legs with his straight razor, her strokes fine and even. She had always been good at that, teasing him in the early days when he worried that she would cut herself.

Time was moving and he was growing frantic. If she could hear him, if he could touch her, stop her, anything . . .

"Claire, please don't do this," he said, trying to make her hear; she carried on, oblivious. "We don't have to stay here, we can go somewhere else." Gentle stroke after gentle stroke, wanting to look her best. He should have done this, should have said these words to her, should have taken the actions that would have made a difference. Earth was not the best place to live, but it would have been better than this. "Another place, anywhere you want to go, just don't do this. I've been so—"

Reality blinked and he swayed on his feet, trying to keep up, trying to make it stop. More water was running, a bathtub filling with steaming water. She sat by the tub as it filled, idly testing the water with her fingers.

"Oh God, Claire, *no*!" he screamed, but she did not hear him, could not see him. He seemed to be watching through glass, unable to go far enough to have an effect. "I'm pleading with you, please, please don't . . ." Tears streamed down his face. He had not known he had so much emotion in him. *Yet who would have thought the old man to have had so much blood in him?* "Not this, not again, please, I've been—"

Reality blinked and his soul twisted.

The razor touched her wrist, slid down and along. Blood flowed freely, like running water. Then the other wrist, harder this time, difficult holding the razor in the left hand, especially now.

The razor dropped to the floor.

Reality blinked and he was standing by the bathtub, looking down at her, her hair floating in a wreath around her pale face. The water had turned a deep shade of red. Claire was gone.

Gone.

He was alone.

He fell to his knees, weeping.

"I've been so alone," he whispered, "so alone . . ."

"Billy," she said, and reality blinked.

He looked up. Now she was standing in front of him. The Core rose behind her, a dark setting for her pale, wet body.

He fell against her, his face burning with the radiant cold from her belly. Pain shook him, tumultuous and terrible. His weeping turned to enormous sobs, grief and terror mingling.

She touched his face, her fingers burning, stroking.

He looked up.

"It's all right," she said, "it's all right. You'll never be alone again. You're with me now, you're with me, and I have such wonderful things to show you. . . ."

She touched his cheek.

Gently, her cold fingers reached for his eyes.

Reality blinked.

Weir raised his hands to his eyes. His nails sank into the flesh, tearing. Blood streamed down his face.

He began to scream, releasing the pain, the anguish, the terror.

The rage.

I am Death, the Destroyer of Worlds. . . .

Exultant, he was reborn.

Chapter Forty-four

Cooper hung head-down over the ad hoc weld on the baffle plate, making one last check for flaws. As far as he could tell, everything here was just, well, peachy. So he was a perfectionist. *And Smith can kiss my happy ass*, he thought.

"Solid as a rock," he said aloud.

Smith, being a pain in the ass and an intrusion into the sacred space of his helmet, said, "How much longer you gonna take, Cooper? I want to get out of here."

Cooper sighed. Smith could be such a humorless dork at times. "Zip that shit," he said. "I'm done. Let me secure my tools, be two minutes, tops."

"Roger that," Smith said, and cut the connection.

Shithead, Cooper thought sourly. He had better be careful what he said—in the end Smith was the one getting them home.

Done with Cooper, Smith turned his attention to unloading CO_2 scrubbers, wondering where Peters had got to. If she did not show up soon, he was going to have to go back to the *Event Horizon* and find her, and that was something he did *not* want to do.

He saw a movement out of the corner of his eye and turned toward it. "Peters," he said, "it's about goddamn time—"

It was Weir, not Peters. Weir had been aboard the *Lewis and Clark*, probably heading out here when the Captain had been calling for them to watch out for the scientist.

Figures it would be my watch, Smith thought. He had had his fill of this mission, of that ship, and of Weir.

Weir ducked around a corner, head down. In a moment he was into the umbilicus, moving like a madman as soon as he hit microgravity.

"Weir, hey, Weir!" Smith shouted. "Get your ass back on board! *Weir!*"

Weir ignored him, spidering up the length of the umbilicus toward the *Event Horizon*.

Smith keyed his radio, furious now. He could have happily throttled Weir. Keeping up with the scientist was turning out to be worse than cat-herding.

"Captain, come in. . . ."

Captain . . ."

Smith on the radio, sounding none too happy. The tone of his voice worried Miller. He slowed from the fast jog he had been maintaining along the *Event Horizon*'s main corridor and found an intercom panel, keying it on.

"Go ahead, Smith," he said.

"I just saw Weir messing around on the *Clark*," Smith said.

Miller sighed. *What the hell is he up to now?*

Something popped and hissed nearby, and Miller turned his head to see. Overhead, crudely severed, stripped wires were touching an exposed electronic circuit, shorting out with a small shower of sparks. It looked as though something had been yanked roughly out of that spot.

He shook his head, starting to turn back to the intercom.

A small box, closer to the floor, caught his eye, the explosives symbol standing out.

He turned to the intercom. "Smith, get out of there."

"Come again, Captain?" Smith sounded startled.

"One of the explosives is missing from the corridor." He

looked up again. The wiring was still shorting out. "Weir could have put it on the *Clark*."

Smith took a step back, going cold. *That son of a bitch!*

"Get off the *Clark* now and wait for me at the main airlock," Miller said.

"No, no, we just got her back together," Smith moaned.

"Get out of there now!" Miller snapped.

You know I can't do that, Captain, Smith thought, bolting from the airlock and racing into the *Lewis and Clark*. There would not be much time, but maybe there was enough. If he could get the charge out into space, away from the ship, most of the explosive force would be wasted, shrapnel being the only problem then.

He ran into the crew quarters, trying to figure out where the scientist could have put the case, ripping open lockers and spilling their contents to the floor.

"Where is it . . . ?" he muttered, emptying Peters' locker, sending her vid unit flying, not caring how much damage he did. Peters could get mad at him later. "Where *is* it?"

Smith?" Miller was yelling at the intercom, but Smith was not answering him. *The stupid, crazy bastard!* "Smith! Fuck!" He smashed his fist into the intercom panel, then turned and ran down the corridor, heading for the airlock, heading for his ship.

He was going to be too late, he knew it.

Smith plowed on through the *Lewis and Clark*. He pulled open a storage locker, started to reach in.

Something was beeping.

"I gotcha!" he said, and started pulling out the contents of the locker. "I gotcha!"

Almost ecstatic, he grabbed a duffel bag that was sitting on the floor, yanking it out. The beeping was louder, clearer. He quickly opened the bag, letting clothing fall to the floor.

The explosive charge was nestled in the clothing like a wicked uncle's idea of an Easter egg, a warning light on top blinking in time with the beeps. The flashing and beeping had grown more rapid in the past seconds—the charge was reaching the end of its countdown.

The beeps stopped. A steady tone sounded.

Smith sat back, closing his eyes and sighing.

No time to prepare to—

Miller raced into the airlock bay.

Thunder rumbled through the air, and he screamed in negation even as the thunder faded and a wave of heat and light slammed him back into the corridor.

Klaxons sounded and he could hear the sound of pressure doors slamming as he tried to pick himself up from the deck.

Through the windows, white light had momentarily replaced the blue of Neptune.

The explosion was silent in the vacuum, opening out of the *Lewis and Clark*'s midsection like a flower of light. The force of the blast tore the ship into two ragged pieces, the drive section spinning away with fuel trailing and flaring, the forward section beginning a slow tumble as it passed over the *Event Horizon*.

Cooper clung desperately to a stanchion, praying that none of the shrapnel from the blast would puncture his suit.

The *Event Horizon* receded into the distance.

Miller walked slowly forward, staring through the airlock bay windows as pieces of his ship tumbled away. Metal shards struck the window, bounced off, leaving no more than minute scratches.

The drive section was tumbling into Neptune's atmosphere. He doubted it would be long before it detonated, providing that enough fuel remained.

The nose section had tumbled past the *Event Horizon* and out of sight.

His ship was dead.

His crew was dying.

Miller turned and walked slowly to an intercom. He keyed it, turning so that he could see the drive section falling.

"DJ," he said, his voice soft with his grief and rage.

"What's happened?" DJ said.

"The *Clark*'s gone." There was a flash of white light. The drive section was disintegrating. "Smith and Cooper are dead. It was Weir. You see him, you take him out."

DJ had finished tidying up in Medical, downloading the med logs and getting his equipment in shape. Now he stood by the intercom, frozen, rage slowly rising as he considered Weir's actions.

"Understood," he said, finally. He was capable of killing, especially when the target was murderously insane.

"Be careful," Miller said.

"I can take care of Weir," DJ said.

He turned around, intending to look for a reasonable weapon.

Weir was waiting for him, smiling. His face was covered in dried blood, his eye sockets nothing more than two bloody holes, still oozing a little.

DJ started to scream, but Weir's red right hand slammed into his throat, silencing him. Pain flared into his head.

There was an odd sound from DJ, muffled by the intercom.

Something crashing, like steel and glass falling to the deck.

Weir.

DJ kicked, fighting away from Weir, but it was no use. Weir tore at him with a terrifying strength, his lack of eyes no handicap. DJ was picked up, slammed into an examination table, picked up again, sent flying through the air, smashed helplessly into storage cabinets.

Weir strode through the carnage, bending down to pick DJ up. The doctor stared up at his tormenter, blood on his lips.

Weir smiled.

He turned DJ around, pulled back his head.

DJ closed his eyes.

In a swift, exact motion, Weir cut DJ's throat from ear to ear, letting the blood spray for a few moments.

He released the corpse, putting aside the scalpel he had used, and turned his attention to cabinets filled with surgical instruments. From one he took surgical needles. From another he took thread.

Sitting down to work, he began threading a needle.

Miller was still trying to get a response over the intercom. Frantic, he changed the channel, keyed it again.

"DJ? DJ, come in."

The intercom hissed.

"I told you," Weir said, his voice soft and strange. "She won't let you leave."

Miller swore and ran out of the airlock bay.

Chapter Forty-five

Miller raced through the *Event Horizon*, driven beyond exhaustion, knowing that if he survived now, he would pay for his efforts.

He reached Medical, barely allowed the hatch time to open.

He stopped, staring.

"DJ," he whispered, staring. "Oh God."

There was blood everywhere, trays toppled, instruments scattered.

DJ had been suspended in a cocoon of bandages and surgical tape, hanging over an operating table at the far end of the medical bay. His throat gaped open.

Miller walked closer.

DJ's midsection had been opened neatly. He had been eviscerated, his organs placed in an orderly fashion on the open surface of the table.

Miller fled from Medical, his mind blurring. Somewhere, he found a tool locker with a nailgun inside, a poor tool overall, but functional enough for killing Weir.

Resolution clearing his mind, he set off for the bridge.

* * *

Cooper figured he was either shaking off the panic and terror or falling into complete hysteria when it occurred to him that there were surfers back on Earth who would kill to get this sort of ride. *Would have curled my hair if it wasn't already.*

Then he was back in the world, ready to deal with the problem at hand. Smith was gone, that much he knew from the radio transmissions. The crazy bastard had tried to get the bomb off the ship, against Miller's orders.

It was, Cooper decided, a mess.

The *Event Horizon* was in the distance now. The wreckage of the *Lewis and Clark*'s front section had passed over the starship and away from Neptune. The orbit would stabilize eventually and then start decaying. Given the location of the bomb, he figured that the drive section had been kicked back toward Neptune and was most likely vaporized by now.

Time to go.

He oriented himself carefully, trying to avoid pushing himself away from the wreckage. His boots clamped firmly to the hull plates. First step, or lack of it. He breathed out, hard, shaky.

He looked at the readout for his air tanks. This was the critical factor now. He was reading one tank full and one tank at half pressure. Relief flooded through him. He could do it.

Carefully, he got his backpack pulled around. This was the *really* tricky part. Working quickly but carefully, he closed one of the main valves, shutting off the full tank. The readout flickered and told him he was on his reserve air supply.

He disconnected the hose from the main tank, unhooked it and pulled it out. He eased his backpack into place again.

He wrapped himself around the full tank, reaching for the valve as he oriented himself to the receding *Event Horizon*. This trick had worked for some people in spaceside training, but not for others. It was popular in the Big Rock Range too, where assorted gasses were easy to extract from the asteroids.

He opened the valve, cutting his boot magnets off. Air puffed from the valve, misted, liquefied, froze. He began to move toward the *Event Horizon*, gathering speed, leaving a crystal trail pointing to where he had been.

The remains of the *Lewis and Clark* spun silently on.

Miller stalked toward the hatchway that led into the bridge, the nailgun feeling hot in his fist.

The hatch was open.

Slowly, he stepped inside, looking left and right.

Someone was sitting at the helm, apparently staring out of the main bridge windows. He raised the nailgun, ready to fire.

Hesitated.

"Weir," he said. His voice was flat and dead.

No movement. He moved forward, slowly, ready to open fire with a hail of rivets. He could barely breathe.

He moved around the helm position, looking over the nailgun.

Not Weir. It was Starck, wired into the helm flight chair, legs pulled back, her wrists bound to them, wire wrapped around her throat to keep her head up though she was unconscious. Blood trickled from her throat where the wire was cutting in. Even in the gloom, Miller could see that she was becoming cyanotic from the slow strangulation.

"Hold on," he whispered, kneeling down and putting the nailgun on the floor, within reach. "Get you out of these . . ."

He was going to space the crazy bastard, that he swore, shove him out of an airlock and watch him die in vacuum. Even that was better than he deserved.

He worked at the wire, cutting his fingers, but managing to undo the binding around her throat. Starck suddenly breathed in, a great painful gasping noise that startled him. He set to work on her arms and her ankles, freeing her, trying to stay aware of the bridge around him.

Starck opened her eyes, moved an arm, stared at him, stared past him, her eyes widening.

Miller turned, knowing he was too vulnerable.

Weir was behind him, appearing with the silence and skill of a ghost. His eyes had been sewn shut, black lines of thread clumsily zigzagging across his eyelids. Lines of dried blood coated his cheeks and chin, marred his flight suit. His hands were blood-red.

Starck lunged sideways, trying for the nailgun. Weir moved like greased lightning, hitting Starck so hard that the navigator was hurled across the bridge, into a bulkhead, stunning her. In the same move, before Miller could do anything about it, Weir snatched up the nailgun, aiming it at Miller's head, then shifting his aim to Miller's right eye.

Miller rose, backed away. "Your eyes . . ." he whispered.

"I don't need them anymore," Weir said. His voice was a cracked curiosity, light with perverse humor, the undertones dark and demonic. This was more than madness, Miller thought. Weir had taken the same road that Kilpack had gone down. "Where we're going, we won't need eyes to see."

"What are you talking about?" Miller said.

"Do you know what a singularity is, Miller? Can your mind truly fathom what a black hole is?" Sightless, he watched Miller. He smiled slightly. "It is *nothing*. Absolute and eternal *nothing*. And if God is everything, then I have seen the Devil." He grinned broadly, spreading his arms joyfully. "It's a liberating experience."

The nailgun swung back to point at Miller's eye. Weir reached out with his free hand, tapped pads, flipped a switch. Displays lit up.

Words appeared on one of the screens, pristine text against a dark background: *Gravity drive is now primed. Do you wish to engage?*

"What are you doing?" Miller said.

"You'll see," Weir said. He grinned again, reached out and tapped a key. He lowered the nailgun again, barely paying attention to Miller.

New text appeared on the display: *Gravity drive engaged. Activation in T-minus ten minutes.* A countdown timer appeared, running backwards.

Miller started a lunge for the nailgun in Weir's hand. It snapped up again. He backed away carefully. "If you miss me, you'll blow out the hull. You'll die too."

"What makes you think I'll miss?" Weir said.

He has a point there, Miller thought.

Something moved at the edge of the bridge windows. Miller had to work hard to cover his shock. Cooper had just drifted into view, peering into the bridge. Miller could barely believe it. If he could keep Weir distracted—

Weir turned so fast that he seemed to blur. The nailgun made a loud spitting sound. A six centimeter nail struck the thick quartz glass of the bridge windows, buried up to the head. A web of minute cracks radiated out from the impact point. Miller could hear the glass creaking.

Weir seemed oblivious to the effects of what he was doing. He stepped toward the window, the nailgun held out.

Cooper suddenly vanished from the window, leaving behind a crystalline trail. Miller almost smiled. Cooper was a resourceful cuss, that was for sure.

Miller turned and ran, diving for the door, hitting the deck and rolling through.

Behind him there was the sound of the nailgun firing and the smack of a nail going into the window. Miller turned around, rising.

Weir turned to look at Miller.

The bridge window shattered, the pieces pouring outward with the atmosphere of the bridge. A gale plucked at Miller, trying to take him from his feet. He managed to grab hold of the door frame, pinning himself in place.

Weir was picked up by the rush of escaping atmosphere, slammed into the helm console and bounced up toward the shattered window as he flailed, trying to grab hold of something, the nailgun falling from his hand and flying out of the window.

Miller's nose was beginning to bleed.

The pressure door was moving.

Weir spread out like a starfish, somehow getting hold of the shattered edges of the bridge window, heedless of the glass chopping into his hands. He started to haul himself back inside, bloody ice forming on his hands and face.

One of the less secure bridge monitors ripped free of its mountings, sailing towards the window, slamming into Weir's midriff. The scientist flailed wildly, trying to regain his grip, but it was too late. Trailing bloody crystals, Weir vanished.

Starck was conscious again, clinging to the side of a console, losing her battle against the outrushing atmosphere. The *Event Horizon* had a lot of atmosphere to dump.

"Come on!" he yelled to Starck, hoping his voice would carry.

"I . . . I can't," she shouted back. Her hands were slipping and she was gasping for air, blood starting to stream from her nose.

Miller turned, grabbing the first almost-loose item that he saw, some kind of compressor unit just outside the bridge. With a yell of desperation, he yanked it loose, slamming it down in the path of the pressure door. Straddling it and putting a hand on the door to help keep it propped open, he leaned into the bridge, holding his other hand out to Starck.

"Give me your hand!" he screamed. "Your hand!"

Starck lunged toward him, reaching out. He closed his hand around hers. The temperature was dropping rapidly, cold enough now to form a layer of ice on their arms. Their veins were bulging as the pressure continued to drop. He did not want to think about the level of capillary damage they were both experiencing.

The door jerked forward in its track, pushing him, crumpling the compressor slightly.

"The door," Starck yelled. "It'll cut you in half! Let go! Let me go!"

"I'm not leaving you," Miller yelled, and he hauled back with all the strength he had left, pulling her back with him into the corridor. As she came she kicked the compressor, loosening it.

Starck fell on top of him, screaming, and he rolled desperately, trying to get them up against a wall.

The compressor pulled free, flew toward the window.

The pressure door slammed shut, almost taking Miller's boot heel.

The winds died down.

Miller gasped for breath, cradling Starck. They were alive, battered, and half-frozen, but they had made it and Weir had not.

In the depths of the ship, a Klaxon began to sound.

Chapter Forty-six

"The forward airlock," Miller said. His lungs hurt beyond belief, drowning the pains in the rest of his body. Starck looked like hell.

They got to their feet, making the best speed they could to Airlock Bay 4, deep in the nose of the ship. It could be Cooper, but there was no way of knowing yet. He had no idea what Weir might be capable of—for all they knew, he might consider an involuntary unsuited spacewalk to be no more than lighthearted fun.

They ran into the airlock bay, coming to a stop. The dim light was no help and the flashing light inside the airlock did nothing but confuse things. All Miller could see was a humanoid shape, moving slowly as it came in.

Miller crossed the Bay, opening a tool cabinet, taking down a zero-g bolt-cutter. It made a more than adequate bludgeon.

"It can't be him," Starck said.

"I'm not taking any chances," Miller said, hefting the bolt-cutter as he walked towards the airlock. "Stay behind me."

The airlock hissed open abruptly.

Cooper tumbled in, frantically trying to remove his helmet.

"Cooper!" Starck shouted. She ran to him, opened the clasps, pulling his helmet off. He bent double, his hands on his knees as he took a deep breath of the dank air and started coughing.

He straightened up, trying for another deep breath. "Let me breathe," he gasped, "let me breathe." Cooper must have been down to the wire when he started back, Miller realized.

"You're okay now," Starck said. "It's over."

"It's not over," Miller said.

Starck turned, following Miller's look. A workstation was active, a display flashing. *Gravity drive engaged. Activation: 00:06:43:01*

"Weir activated the drive. We've got to shut it down."

Cooper glanced at the workstation, looked back at Weir. "How? The bridge—"

"The bridge is gone," Starck said. "What about Engineering?"

Miller gave her a hard look. "Can you shut it down?"

"I don't know the process," Starck said angrily. "Dr. Weir was the expert."

"I don't want to go where the last crew went," Cooper said, giving Miller an unwavering look. "I'd rather be dead."

"Then we blow the fucker up," Miller said.

"Blow it up?" Starck said, staring at him as though he had followed Weir into the mouth of madness.

Miller went over to the workstation, the others following. He keyed in commands, pulling up a schematic of the ship, pointing. "We blow the corridor. Like Weir said: use the foredecks as a life boat, separate it from the rest of the ship. We stay put—"

"And the gravity drive goes where no man has gone before," Cooper said, his eyes narrowing.

He did not smile.

Chapter Forty-seven

They entered the Gravity Couch Bay at a trot. Justin was still floating comfortably in his tank, unperturbed by the recent events. Miller was grateful for that—Justin had been spared some of this insanity.

Miller stopped and turned. "You prep the Gravity Couches. I'm going to manually arm those explosives."

"Will this shit work?" Cooper said.

"It worked for Weir," Miller said. He doubted anyone was in the mood for ironic comments. "Prep the tanks."

Starck stepped toward him. "I'll go with you—"

"Just get those tanks ready," he said, moving toward the hatchway. He nodded at the hatch. "Close it behind me. Just in case."

Starck stared at Miller for a long moment, as though trying to burn his face into her memory. "Miller . . ."

"Be right back," he said, attempting a reassuring, confident tone and knowing that he was failing miserably.

He smiled, knowing it to be false, and stepped through the hatch. She stared at him for a moment longer, then reached to her right.

The hatch closed with a dull sound and he was alone.

He took a deep breath and ran.

He made it to the central corridor in record time, hurtling along it as though trying to break every sprinting record in the book. Reaching a coupling, he dropped quickly to one knee, reaching down to pop the catches on the cover of an explosive charge.

He lifted the cover off. There was an unlit indicator on the charge, and a single switch. One of the switch positions was labeled MANUAL in bold letters.

Leaving the cover off, he went to the next charge, repeating the process, hurrying as much as he dared. They were almost out of time. . . .

Chapter Forty-eight

Cooper and Starck went down the rows of Gravity Couches, checking each one, opening them, closing them again, checking the display panels. As long as everything worked in the life suspension systems, they were in fine shape. On this trip they did not need to worry about the state of the inertial dampers—they were unlikely to be picking up much in the way of thrust.

"I'm gonna activate the emergency beacon," Cooper said.

"Hurry," Starck said. All things considered, she did not want to spend any time alone, not now.

Cooper grabbed a flashlight from an open locker and pulled open a floor access panel. He peered down into the access tube, then sat down on the edge, lowering himself into it. She watched him vanish, then turned back to her work, going over to the main workstation.

It was a redundant check, but it still needed to be done. She activated three of the empty Gravity Couches, watching the readouts to confirm the proper rate of gel flow into the tanks. So far so good.

Behind her, two of the tanks began to fill with green gel.

* * *

In Medical and on the ruined bridge, the bio-scans were going wild again, off the scale, the electronics distorting the data to try and make it fit within the parameters their designers had set.

In the Second Containment, the Core darkened, rippling as energy built up within it. Dark lightning curled around it, reaching out to the control spikes.

Reality ran like water.

Behind Starck, something thudded against the side of one of the Gravity Couches, startling her out of her focus on the workstation. Before she could turn around, the sound came again.

She expected to see Cooper, back from belowdecks.

She stared for a long moment. Two of the Gravity Couches had filled with green gel, but the third was darker, more liquid. If she hadn't known better, she would have thought that the liquid was blood, but it could not be.

Somewhere in the system, there had been a fluid containment failure, allowing the gel to degrade. She would have to drain the tank and activate another one.

There seemed to be something moving in the tank. Slowly, she walked over to it, trying to focus, trying to figure out what could have gotten into the fluid. She had never heard of this sort of gel breakdown before, but Gravity Couches were not her area of expertise by far.

She leaned toward the tank.

Another low thud.

A face pressed up against the glass of the tank, grinning at her.

Weir.

She screamed, backing away. Weir's face had not finished forming yet, the skin incomplete, the white of bone showing through, muscle tissue flexing as he worked his jaw.

"Cooper!" she screamed.

The tank exploded in a torrent of glass shards and thick blood.

Weir, still grinning, still forming, came for her.

*   *   *

Cooper crouched in the access tunnel beneath the Gravity Couch Bay, working his way along the circuit panels, finally locating the breaker that controlled power to the emergency beacon. It had somehow been fused open.

Working quickly, he rigged a bypass, restoring power. The panel in front of him lit up like a bad night in Las Vegas. It would take hours yet, but USAC would eventually pick up the distress beacon.

He closed the panel and backed up.

Something wet and sticky struck his shoulder, soaking into his flight suit. He turned his head, shocked, looked up. Blood was running in a rivulet along the ceiling, dripping at intervals.

He started back toward the vertical access.

"Starck?" he called. Blood was splashing into the access tunnel, far too much of it to be from one single person. "Starck?"

He reached the ladder, moving cautiously to look upward.

Starck fell, almost catching herself on the ladder, losing her grip. She was covered in blood. She landed awkwardly on the deck, rolled over, tried to get to her feet. Cooper bent to help her.

"Run!" she screamed at him, shoving him away.

He looked up.

Weir oozed into the vertical access, staring down at them, coming headfirst down the ladder like a gigantic spider. He hissed as he moved. Cooper saw raw muscle, distorted tissue.

Cooper ran. The Hellhound had arrived.

Starck, staggering, came after him.

Chapter Forty-nine

Miller knelt, opening the last of the charges, flipping the switch. This was the important one, marked with a red radio sigil. There was a second switch inside the container. He flipped it. A small cover popped open.

Carefully, he reached inside and removed a small radio detonator. This system had been built with fail-safes in mind, granting the possibility that the computer-controlled systems might be offline or destroyed. In an emergency the *Event Horizon's* crew could have made it home to Earth, given that they were still within this solar system, or to landfall on any seemingly hospitable planet.

There were two buttons on the radio detonator, one green, one red. He pressed the green button.

Red lights glowed through the gloom of the corridor, marking the location of the couplings. He was almost down at the First Containment now. He would be racing the clock to get back to the Gravity Couch Bay before the gravity drive activated.

He found an intercom panel, keyed it. "We're armed, she's ready to blow," he said. "Repeat, we are armed."

There was no reply from the intercom. "Starck, you copy? Cooper?"

He swore under his breath. The only thing he could do now was run like hell and hope he made it.

He turned.

The corridor flared with red light, and heat washed over him.

The burning man had returned, filling the corridor with fire from wall to wall, blocking Miller's escape.

"*You left me behind,*" the burning man hissed, his voice crackling and popping like flaring tinderwood.

"Corrick . . ." Miller said, afraid.

"*I begged you. I begged you to save me.*"

"I couldn't," Miller said. Was there any hope that Corrick would ever understand? Did it matter? In his heart, he had always expected that amends would someday be due. "Do you think I didn't want to?"

"*You abandoned me. You stood there and did* nothing." The voice crackled with anger and the flames brightened momentarily. The heat was threatening to suffocate Miller.

"That's not true!" Miller screamed.

"*You let me* burn!" The flames were almost white as the burning figure howled, the howl becoming a terrible scream of rage and accusation.

The burning man pointed. Fire poured around him, liquid and swift, flowing over the walls, the floor, the ceiling.

Miller turned and ran frantically into the First Containment. An alarm shrieked. The flames were almost at his heels, chasing him like something alive as he fled into the separator and toward the Second Containment.

The main door to the Second Containment was closing, either in answer to the Core, or in response to the flames. He pushed harder, dove headlong through the remaining gap, skinning his side on the door. The floor here was slick with coolant, and he could not get his balance. He slammed into the main workstation console, fetching up hard.

The door was not quite closed. Flames gouted through the tiny opening, spewing towards him. He rolled aside, covering his head, feeling the heat of the fire going past him.

The console exploded, showering him with hot plastic and metal, parts splashing into the coolant and ricocheting from the bulkheads and the door.

He looked up. The door was shut firmly now. The paint on it bubbled with the heat from the other side, darkening.

Miller stood up, carefully. He looked at the detonator in his hand, shaking his head. They were about out of time, and he regretted his reassurance to Starck. She would get Cooper and herself taken care of, no matter what.

He was afraid of where he was going.

Red light washed over him again, and his shadow grew tall in front of him.

He turned, expecting to see his latest adversary. He took an involuntary step backward, shocked at the sight that greeted him.

The Second Containment was a fury of fire, a wall-to-wall holocaust, fire flowing over the control spikes, over the surfaces, pouring through the air. The Core glowed cherry red, orange, its color shifting through blazing white, a small, corrupt sun in the heart of chaos.

"*Don't leave me!*"

He turned toward the crackling voice. The burning man was beside him. Miller started to back away, but he was not fast enough. The burning man swung his arm, smashing it into Miller.

Miller tumbled and slid, his clothes burning, his hair singed. He fell into the coolant, losing the detonator as he struck the deck. His head went under the muck and coolant went into his mouth, tasting foul.

He rolled over and pushed himself up, spitting coolant out, choking from the taste, trying not to vomit. The coolant had at least doused the flames on his clothes.

The burning man was walking toward him, the coolant bubbling and steaming where his feet came down.

Miller knew, now, knew the truth, or at least some of the truth. There had been just too much . . .

"*Look at me!*" the burning man commanded, but Miller was not having any of that now.

Facing the burning man, Miller shouted, "No! You're not

Edmund Corrick. I know you're not . . . because I saw him *die!*''

The burning man stopped.

The flames faded away, leaving only a ghost of heat. The Second Containment was dark, humming with the power that was building.

William Weir stood before him now, but this was not the Weir he knew. The body was larger, misshapen. The face was Weir's, but the skin appeared to have the texture of wood. Runes had been etched into Weir's forehead and cheeks.

The monster had *eyes*. They glittered green, too large, too deep. There was a reptilian coldness there, a look that spoke of millions of years. The creature had some of Weir's form, but it reeked of an alien nature that left Miller with a sense of horror that transcended anything he had ever felt.

"Weir?" he said.

"Weir is gone," the creature said, but its voice was remarkably like that of the scientist. "The poor fool. He was reaching for the heavens, but all he found was *me*."

Miller stared, forcing himself past his reactions. "Well, what the fuck are you?"

"You know what I am."

Without thinking, Miller swung, a right cross that the creature caught easily. Miller screamed as his fist was slowly crushed. Long nails cut into his flesh and blood ran.

The creature hurled him away, into a bulkhead. Something cracked in Miller's side, and he slid down, sitting in the coolant, stunned, barely able to breathe.

The creature walked slowly toward him. "I am your confessor." It bent to look at him, tilting its head. "Confess your sins to me. I feel the weight of Edmund Corrick's death inside you."

Miller raised his head. "What do you want from me?" He was weary. He wished this would be over.

"Respect," the creature said, crouching to face him. "The reverence I deserve. Or did you think you could profane this place without it coming to my attention? Did you think you could come pounding on my door and I would not answer?"

"Why don't you just kill me and get it over with?" Miller hissed.

The creature grinned. "Kill you? I don't want you dead. Just the opposite. I want you to live forever." The creature reached out to him, grasping his head. Miller struggled, twisting. He could not break the creature's grasp. "Let me show you."

Miller screamed.

Images cascaded through his mind, horrific, endless. In moments he saw the bloody fates of the original crew, saw them torn apart, degraded, destroyed from within and without. He was drowning in blood and suffering, too much of it for him to accept, too much to withstand.

"Do you see?" the creature asked, its parody of Weir's voice almost a caress.

Miller writhed, trying to break the contact, trying to make the horror stop.

His hand struck something under the surface of the coolant. The pain jarred him free of the cascade of images for a moment, long enough. He reached down, grasping, found a familiar handle. A CO_2 scrubber, dropped by either Smith or Peters.

The visions surged back, swirling through his mind.

"Do you see?" the creature whispered.

He saw. Justin, Starck, and Cooper had been crucified upside-down over the Core, blood dripping from their bodies.

"No!" Miller cried, thrashing. "They're not dead! You didn't get them!"

"Not yet," the creature said. "Soon. Very soon."

"*No!*" Miller screamed.

He thrashed around again, and this time his head came away from the creature's hands. He sank beneath the coolant for a moment, then surged up, bringing the CO_2 scrubber up and around, slamming it into the creature's head.

The creature staggered back, shaking its head, blinking.

Miller came to his feet. "Leave them alone!"

He swung the scrubber again, with all the force he could muster, snapping the creature's head around, making it stagger. He saw blood pouring from an open wound, filling the runes.

"Hurts, doesn't it?" Miller screamed at the creature, letting the fury take him over. He swung the scrubber back and forth, scything, each blow sending the creature staggering back.

He swung again.

The creature reached up, snatching the scrubber out of the air, ripping it from Miller's hands, hurling it away. In a blur, it had Miller, too, lifting him, flinging him into the coolant.

Miller slammed into the deck, coolant washing over him. Pain flooded his body from head to foot. He knew things were broken, ribs, organs, there had to be internal bleeding.

He could not move.

The creature stood over him. An improbably long tongue eeled out of its mouth, licking at the bloody runes on its face. It smacked its lips, pleased. "Yes," it hissed. "I had forgotten how good that can taste."

Miller lay in the coolant, moaning.

The creature squatted over him. "You should be flattered I've taken an interest in you. Weir, the others . . . they were easy. But you will *fight*."

Beyond the creature, the Core was a deepening darkness, swelling outward. All around, the control rods were moving. Darkness seemed to be filling the universe.

Dark fire flashed through the runes on the creature's face, traveled down the length of its body, revealing more runes, intricately woven together.

"You will struggle against me with every ounce of strength you possess . . . right up to the moment when you surrender to me willingly."

"Don't count on it," Miller hissed through clenched teeth.

His fingers touched something small, hard in the coolant.

A great deep rumbling filled the Second Containment. The control rods were entering the Core now.

Hoping blindly, Miller closed his hand.

"I don't ask you to embrace me with blind faith," the creature said, softly. "I will win you."

Will you now? Miller rolled over, getting to all fours, trying to get to his feet. *It's time*, he thought, *time to go*.

The creature kicked out.

Miller slid again, pushing a bow wave of coolant ahead of himself. Pale fire ripped through him. At this rate he would not last much longer.

Sorry, Starck, so sorry, he thought.

He tried to rise again, and could not complete his movement. He fell back into the muck.

In the distance, the Core swelled, its humming reaching a crescendo. Energy pulsed forth, along the control rods, rippling along the surfaces of the walls.

The creature came down to him.

Through a red haze of pain, Miller said, "You want me to pay for . . . mistakes?"

"I want to reward you for them," the creature said, smiling. It was a mass of brilliant runes now, growing stronger as the Core continued its progress.

Reality had melted around the Core, the walls shifting, changing, vanishing, becoming part of the Core's intolerable blackness. The universe was being swallowed by the heart of this ship.

The Core grew, screaming.

"You want me to burn in hell?" Miller said. "You want to take my soul? Sorry, it's not for sale."

The creature was folding its body into a kneeling shape by him. It bent until its face was centimeters from Miller's. He could smell the stink of its breath over everything else.

"I will give you endless days of pain," the creature said, "immeasurable agony. The more profound your despair, the greater will be my pleasure. And, in the end, after all of it . . . you will thank me."

A surge of movement. The creature grasped Miller by the front of his flight suit, lifting him from the coolant, holding him in the air, still eye to eye. Miller glared into the hellish corruption of Weir's face, unwavering.

"Do you see?" the creature said. It was framed by the chaos that had been the Second Containment. "*Do you see?*"

"Yes," Miller said, choosing his destiny there and then, regretting nothing, "I see."

He raised his fist, held it between their faces.

Without irony, he said, "Go to hell."

He pressed the second button.

Chapter Fifty

Starck and Cooper were in a side corridor when the explosive charges went off. The *Event Horizon* seemed to lift and leap forward, pulling free, sending them both tumbling to the deck.

They got up again, made it to a window.

The drive section of the *Event Horizon* had plunged into the atmosphere of Neptune, some of its velocity leeched away by the separation of the foredecks.

A black sphere was growing around the heart of the drive section, swallowing it up, growing. The blue clouds were swirling around it, a whirlpool forming. They were witnessing a black hole forming and working.

The black sphere expanded rapidly, paused as it swallowed the main part of the drive section.

Even more quickly, the black hole shrank, Neptune's clouds becoming ever more agitated the more the Schwarzschild radius contracted. Within a few moments, all that was left was a dark gap in the cloudscape, and even that was being filled in as Neptune's winds worked to erase the scar.

Starck touched the cold quartz of the window, her heart breaking, knowing that her captain would not be coming back. The thing that had been Weir had suddenly abandoned its pursuit of the two of them, scenting more interesting game. She had known that Miller would not be returning, no matter how much of a brave face he had put on.

She leaned against the window while Cooper watched the place where the other half of the *Event Horizon* had been. They would have to get into the Gravity Couches soon, taking their chances that USAC would mount another rescue mission. They might well drift forever, lost.

"Miller . . ." she whispered, watching the clouds fill in the last place he had been.

She turned away.

Chapter Fifty-one

Darkness.

Three beams of light cut through the darkness.

There were three of them, in full EVA gear, their lights playing over the interior of the Gravity Couch Bay, finding the shattered tank, the bloody floor.

Three tanks were occupied. Two males, one female.

One of the astronauts approached Starck's tank, his light shining into her face.

Suddenly, her eyes opened.

She struggled, kicked, panicking. The tank drained rapidly, opened, disgorged her.

She fell to the floor, no strength in her arms and legs.

She looked up, wondering how she could have been seeing things outside of her body while she was unconscious in the tank. She could not speak.

The astronaut bent to help her up.

"You're safe now," he said, gently.

Her mind filled with thoughts of others. "Cooper, is he . . . Justin . . ."

"They're fine, they're with us." The astronaut reached up,

undogged his helmet. "You're all with us now."

He pulled his helmet off.

Weir smiled at her, his darkened face covered with runes, his eyes strange and alien.

"You're with us," he said, softly, reaching for her.

She began to scream.

They had emptied the second tank and gotten the woman, Starck, onto a bio-stretcher, everything going fine until she had opened her eyes and begun screaming for no reason that anyone could see.

The rescue tech ministering to her turned around, yelling, "We need a sedative here!"

Cooper, who had decanted in nothing more than his birthday suit and had yet to put on a stitch of clothing, pushed the rescue tech aside, grabbing Starck's shoulders, trying to get through to her, to comfort her. No one in the rescue team had a clue as to what had taken place here, only that it had been traumatic in nature.

"Starck, it's me," Cooper said, trying to break through her screaming. "It's me, come on now, it's okay, we're okay, we're okay . . ."

But she had seen the face of the beast, and had known it would always be with her.

She continued to scream. . . .